HORROR GEMS

Volume 2

Joseph Payne Brennan
and others

Compiled and Edited by
GREGORY LUCE

ARMCHAIR FICTION
PO Box 4369, Medford, Oregon 97504

For more information about Armchair Books and products, visit our website at…

www.armchairfiction.com

Or email us at…

armchairfiction@yahoo.com

CHILLS, THRILLS AND FANTASTIC DOIN'S...

"The Ghost that Never Died" and "Way Station" show two very different distinctions between here and there...

Nature, and woman, was never really meant to be trifled with as you will see in the tales of "Dr. Adam's Garden of the Evil" and "The Chemical Vampire."

What hideous monstrosities are waiting for us in the dark? "Widow House" and "Mop-Head" may be just the tales to tell you.

In "The Calamander Chest" and "Music of Eric Zann" evil will either draw you toward it or drive you away.

An excellent cache of brilliant writers bound into yet another volume of pure horror. Please, take your time...to enjoy...to scream...or just run madly into the night...

TABLE OF CONTENTS

THE CALAMANDER CHEST

By Joseph Payne Brennan

"FROM the Indies it is, sir!" said the second-hand dealer, pressing his palms together. "Genuine calamander wood—a rare good buy it is, sir!"

"Well—I'll take it," replied Ernest Maax somewhat hesitantly.

He had been strolling rather idly through the antique and second-hand shop when the chest caught his attention. It had a rich, exotic look, which pleased him. In appearance the dark brown, black-striped wood resembled ebony. And the chest was quite capacious. It was at least two feet wide and five feet long, with a depth of nearly three feet. When Maax learned that the dealer was willing to dispose of it for only twelve dollars, he could not resist buying it.

What made him hesitate a little was the dealer's initial low price and quite obvious pleasure upon completing the transaction. Was that fine-grained wood only an inlay, or did the chest contain some hidden defect?

When it was delivered to his room the next day, he could find nothing wrong with it. The calamander wood was solid and sound and the entire chest appeared to be in fine condition. The lid clicked smoothly into place when lowered, and the big iron key turned readily enough.

Feeling quite satisfied with himself, Maax carefully polished the dark wood and then slid the chest into an empty corner of his room. The next time he changed his lodgings, the chest would prove invaluable. Meanwhile it added just the right exotic touch to his rather drab chamber.

Several weeks passed, and although he still cast occasional admiring glances at his new possession, it gradually began to recede from his mind.

Then one evening his attention was returned to it in a very startling manner.

He was sitting up, reading, rather late in the evening, when for some reason his eyes lifted from his book and he looked across the room toward the corner where he had placed the chest.

A long white finger protruded from under its lid.

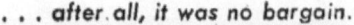

. . . *after all, it was no bargain.*

CALAMANDER CHEST

BY JOSEPH PAYNE BRENNAN

He sat motionless, overwhelmed with sudden horror, his eyes riveted on this appalling object.

It just hung there unmoving, a long pale finger with a heavy knucklebone and a black nail.

After his first shock, Maax felt a slow rage kindling within him. The finger had no right to be there; it was unreasonable—and idiotic. He resented it bitterly, much as he would have resented the sudden intrusion of an unsavory roomer from down the hall. His peaceful, comfortable evening was ruined by this outrageous manifestation.

With an oath, he hurled his book straight at the finger.

It disappeared. At least he could no longer see it. Tilting his reading light so that its beams shot across the room, he strode to the chest and flung open the lid.

There was nothing inside.

Dropping the lid, he picked up his book and returned to the chair. Perhaps, he reflected, he had been reading too much lately. His, eyes, in protest, might be playing tricks on him.

For some time longer he pretended to read, but at frequent intervals he slowly lifted his eyes and looked across the room toward the calamander chest. The finger did not reappear however, and eventually he went to bed.

A WEEK passed and he began to forget about the finger. He stayed out more during the evening, and read less, and by the end of a week he was quite convinced that he had been the victim of nothing more than an odd hallucination brought on by simple eyestrain.

At length, at the beginning of the second week, deciding that his eyes had had a good rest, he bought some current magazines and made up his mind to spend the evening in his room.

Some time after he took up the first magazine, he glanced over at the chest and saw that all was as it should be. Settling comfortably in his chair, he became absorbed in the magazine and did not put it aside for over an hour. As he finally laid it down and prepared to pick up another, his eyes strayed in the direction of the chest—and there was the finger.

It hung there as before, motionless, with its thick knuckle and repulsive black nail.

Crowding down an impulse to rush across the room, Maax slowly reached over to a small table, which stood near his chair and felt for a heavy metal ashtray. As his hand closed on the tray, his eyes never left the finger.

Rising very slowly, he began to inch across the room. He was certain that the ashtray, if wielded with force, would effectively crush anything less substantial than itself, which it descended on. It was made of solid metal, and it possessed a sharp edge.

When he was a scant yard away from the chest, the finger disappeared. When he lifted the lid, the chest, as he had expected, was empty.

Feeling considerably shaken, he returned to his chair and sat down. Although the finger did not reappear, he could not drive its hideous image out of his mind. Before going to bed, he reluctantly decided that he would get rid of the chest.

He was in sound health and his eyes had had a week's rest. Therefore, he reasoned, whatever flaw in nature permitted the ugly manifestation rested not with him but with the chest itself.

Looking back, he recalled the second-hand dealer's eagerness to sell the chest at a ridiculously low price. The thing must already have had an evil reputation when the antique dealer acquired it. Knowing it, the unscrupulous merchant had readily consented to part with it for a small sum.

Maax, a practical young man, admitted the possibility of a nonphysical explanation only with reluctance, but felt that he was not in a position to debate the matter. The preservation of stable nerves came first. All other considerations were secondary.

ACCORDINGLY, on the following day, before leaving for work, he arranged with his landlady to have the chest picked up and carted off to the city dump. He included specific directions that upon arrival it was to be burned.

When he arrived back at his room that evening however, the first thing that met his gaze was the calamander chest. Furious, he hurried down the hall to his landlady's apartment and demanded an explanation. Why had his orders been ignored?

When she was able to get a word in, the patient woman explained that the chest actually had been picked up and carted off to the dump. Upon arrival however, the man in charge of the dump had assured the men who lugged in the chest that there must be some mistake. Nobody in his right mind, he asserted, would destroy such a beautiful and expensive article. The men must have picked up the wrong one; surely there must be another left behind, he said, which was the worthless one the owner wanted discarded.

The two men who had taken the chest to the dump, not feeling secure in their own minds about the matter, and not wishing to make a costly mistake, had returned the chest later in the day.

Completely nonplussed by this information, Maax muttered an apology to the landlady and went back to his room, where he plopped into a chair and sat staring at the chest. He would, he finally decided, give it one more chance. If nothing further happened, he would keep it; otherwise he would take immediate and drastic measures to get rid of it once and for all.

Although he had planned to attend a concert that evening, it began to rain shortly after six o'clock and he resigned himself to an evening in his room.

Before starting to read, he locked the chest with the iron key and put the key in his pocket. It was absurd that he had not thought of doing so before. This would, he felt, be the decisive test.

While he read, he maintained a keen watch on the chest, but nothing happened until well after eleven, when he put aside his book for the evening.

As he closed the book and started to rise, he looked at the chest—and there was the finger. In appearance it was unchanged. Instead of hanging slack and motionless however, it now seemed to be imbued with faint life. It quivered slightly and it appeared to be making weak attempts to scratch the side of the chest with its long black nail.

When he finally summoned up sufficient courage, Maax took up the metal ashtray as before and crept across the room. This time he actually had the tray raised to strike before the finger vanished. It seemed to whisk back into the chest.

With a wildly thumping heart, Maax lifted the lid. Again the box was empty. But then he remembered the iron key in his pocket and a new thrill of horror coursed down his spine. The hideous digital apparition had unlocked the chest! Either that or he was rapidly losing his sanity.

Completely unnerved, he locked the chest for a second time and then sat in a chair and watched it until two o'clock in the morning. At length, exhausted and deeply shaken, he sought his bed. Before putting out the light, he ascertained that the chest was still locked.

As soon as he fell asleep, he experienced a hideous nightmare. He dreamed that a persistent scratching sound woke him up, that he arose, lit a candle, and looked at the chest. The protruding finger showed just under the lid and this time it was galvanized with an excess of life. It twisted and turned, drummed with its thick knuckle, scratched frantically with its flat black nail. At length, as if it suddenly became aware of his presence, it became perfectly still—and then very deliberately beckoned for him to approach. Flooded with horror, he nevertheless found himself unable to disobey. Setting down the candle, he slowly crossed the room like an automaton. The monstrous beckoning finger drew him on like some infernal magnet, which attracted human flesh instead of metal.

As he reached the chest, the finger darted inside and the lid immediately lifted. Overwhelmed with terror and yet utterly unable to stop himself, he stepped into the chest, sat down, drew his knees up to his chin and turned onto his side. A second later the lid slammed shut and he heard the iron key turn in the lock.

At this point in the nightmare he awoke with a ringing scream. He sat up in bed and felt the sweat of fear running down his face. In spite of his nightmare—or because of it—he dared not get up and switch on the light. Instead, he burrowed under the bedclothes and lay wide-awake till morning.

After he had regained some measure of self-composure, he went out for black coffee and then, instead of reporting to his job, rode across town to the modest home of a truck driver and mover whom he had hired at various times in the past. After some quite detailed and specific plans had been agreed upon, he paid the mover ten dollars and departed with a promise to pay him an equal amount when the job was done. After lunch, considerably relieved, he went to work.

HE ENTERED his room that evening with a confident air, but as soon as he looked around, his heart sank. Contrary to instructions, the mover had not picked up the chest. It remained in the corner, just where it had been.

This time Maax was more depressed than angry. He sought out a telephone and called up the mover. The man was profusely apologetic. His truck had broken down, he explained, just as he was starting out to pick up the chest. The repairs were nearly completed however, and he would absolutely be out to carry off the chest the first thing in the morning.

Since there was nothing else he could do, Maax thanked him and hung up. Finding himself unusually reluctant to return to his room, he ate a leisurely dinner at a nearby restaurant and later attended a movie. After the movie he stopped and had a hot chocolate. It was nearly midnight before he got back to his room.

In spite of his nightmare of the previous evening, he found himself looking forward to bed. He had lost almost an entire night's sleep and he was beginning to feel the strain.

After assuring himself that the calamander chest was securely locked, he slipped the iron key under his pillow and got into bed. In spite of his uneasiness he soon fell asleep.

Some hours later he awoke suddenly and sat up. His heart was pounding. For a moment he was not aware of what had awakened him—then he heard it. A furious scratching, tapping, thumping sound came from one corner of the room.

Trembling violently, he got out of bed, crossed the room and pressed the button on his reading lamp. Nothing happened. Either the electricity was shut off or the light bulb had burned out.

He pulled open a drawer of the lamp stand and frantically searched for a candle. By the time he found one and applied a match to its wick, the scratching sound had redoubled in intensity. The entire room seemed filled with it.

Shuddering, he lifted the candle and started across the room toward the calamander chest. As the wavering light of the candle flickered into the far corner, he saw the finger.

It protruded far out of the chest and it was writhing with furious life. It thrummed and twisted, dug at the chest with its horrible black nail, tapped and turned in an absolute frenzy of movement.

Suddenly, as he advanced, it became absolutely still. It hung down limp. Engulfed with terror, Maax was convinced that it had become aware of his approach and was now watching him.

When he was halfway across the room, the finger slowly lifted and deliberately beckoned to him. With a rush of renewed horror Maax remembered the ghastly events of his dream. Yet—as in the nightmare—he found himself utterly unable to disobey that diabolical summons. He continued on like a man in a trance...

EARLY the next morning the mover and his assistant were let into Maax's room by the landlady. Maax had apparently already left for work, but there was no need of his presence since he had already given the mover detailed instructions in regard to the disposal of the chest.

The chest, locked but without a key, stood in one corner of the room. The melted wax remains of a candle, burned to the end of its wick, lay nearby.

The landlady shook her head, "A good way to burn the house down," she complained. "I'll have to speak to Mr. Maax. Not like him to be so careless."

The movers, burdened with the chest, paid no attention to her. The assistant growled as they started down the stairs. "Must be lined with lead. Never knew a chest so heavy before!"

"Heavy wood," his companion commented shortly, not wishing to waste his breath.

"Wonder why he's dumpin' such a good chest?" the assistant asked later as the truck approached an abandoned quarry near the edge of town.

The chief mover glanced at him slyly. "I guess I know," he said. "He bought it of Jason Kinkle. And Kinkle never told him the story on it. But he found out later I figure—and that's why he's pitchin' it."

The assistant's interest picked up. "What's the story?" he asked.

They drove into the quarry grounds and got out of the truck.

"Kinkle bought it dirt cheap at an auction," the mover explained as they lifted out the chest. "Auction of old Henry Stubberton's furniture."

The assistant's eyes widened as they started up a steep slope with the chest. "You mean the Stubberton they found murdered in a…"

"In a chest!" the mover finished for him. *"This chest!"*

Neither spoke again until they set down the chest at the edge of a steep quarry shaft.

Glancing down at the deep water, which filled the bottom of the shaft, the mover wiped the sweat from his face. "A pretty sight they say he was. All doubled up and turnin' black. Seems he wasn't dead when they shut him in though. They say he must have tried to claw his way out! When they opened the chest, they found one of his fingers jammed up under the lid, near the lock! Tried to pick the lock with his fingernail, it looked like!"

The assistant shuddered. "Let's be rid of it then. It's bad luck sure!"

The mover nodded. "Take hold and shove."

They strained together and in another second the calamander chest slipped over the edge of the quarry and hurtled toward the pool of black water far below. There was one terrific splash and then it sank from sight like a stone.

"That's good riddance and another tenner for me," the mover commented.

Oddly enough however, he never collected the tenner, for after that day Mr. Ernest Maax dropped completely out of sight. He was never seen nor heard of again. The disgruntled mover, never on the best of terms with the police, shrugged off the loss of the tenner and neglected to report the disposal of the chest. And since the landlady had never learned the mover's name, or where he intended taking the chest, her sparse information was of no help in the search.

The police concluded that Maax had gotten into some scrape, changed his name, and effected a permanent change of locale.

THE END

THE MUSIC OF ERICH ZANN

By H. P. Lovecraft

I have examined maps of the city with the greatest care, yet have never again found the Rue d'Auseil. These maps have not been modern maps alone, for I know that names change. I have, on the contrary, delved deeply into all the antiquities of the place, and have personally explored every region, of whatever name, which could possibly, answer to the street I knew as the Rue d'Auseil. But despite all I have done, it remains an humiliating fact that I cannot find the house, the street, or even the locality, where, during the last months of my impoverished life as a student of metaphysics at the university, I heard the music of Erich Zann.

That my memory is broken, I do not wonder; for my health, physical and mental, was gravely disturbed throughout the period of my residence in the Rue d'Auseil, and I recall that I took none of my few acquaintances there. But that I cannot find the place again is both singular and perplexing; for it was within a half-hour's walk of the university and was distinguished by peculiarities, which could hardly be forgotten by any one who had been there. I have never met a person who has seen the Rue d'Auseil.

The Rue d'Auseil lay across a dark river bordered by precipitous brick blear-windowed warehouses and spanned by a ponderous bridge of dark stone. It was always shadowy along that river, as if the smoke of neighboring factories shut out the sun perpetually. The river was also odorous with evil stenches which I have never smelled elsewhere, and which may some day help me to find it, since I should recognize them at once. Beyond the bridge were narrow cobbled streets with rails; and then came the ascent, at first gradual, but incredibly steep as the Rue d'Auseil was reached.

I have never seen another street as narrow and steep as the Rue d'Auseil. It was almost a cliff, closed to all vehicles, consisting in several places of flights of steps, and ending at the top in a lofty ivied wall. Its paving was irregular, sometimes stone slabs, sometimes cobblestones, and sometimes bare earth with struggling greenish-grey vegetation. The houses were tall, peaked-roofed, incredibly old, and crazily leaning backward, forward, and sidewise. Occasionally an opposite pair, both leaning forward, almost met across the street like an arch; and certainly they kept most of the light from the ground below. There were a few overhead bridges from house to house across the street.

The inhabitants of that street impressed me peculiarly. At first I thought it was because they were all silent and reticent; but later decided it was because they were all very old. I do not know how I came to live on such a street, but I was not myself when I moved there. I had been living in many poor places, always evicted for want of money; until at last I came upon that tottering house in the Rue d'Auseil kept by the paralytic Blandot. It was the third house from the top of the street, and by far the tallest of them all.

My room was on the fifth story; the only inhabited room there, since the house was almost empty. On the night I arrived I heard strange music from the peaked garret overhead, and the next day asked old Blandot about it. He told me it was an old German viol-player, a strange dumb man who signed his name as Erich Zann, and who played evenings in a cheap theater orchestra; adding that Zann's desire to play in the night after his return from the theater was the reason he had chosen this lofty and isolated garret room, whose single gable window was the only point on the street from which one could look over the terminating wall at the declivity and panorama beyond.

Thereafter I heard Zann every night, and although he kept me awake, I was haunted by the weirdness of his music. Knowing little of the art myself, I was yet certain that none of his harmonies had any relation to music I had heard before; and concluded that he was a composer of highly original genius. The longer I listened, the more I was fascinated, until after a week I resolved to make the old man's acquaintance.

One night as he was returning from his work, I intercepted Zann in the hallway and told him that I would like to know him and be with him when he played. He was a small, lean, bent person, with shabby clothes, blue eyes, grotesque, satyr-like face, and nearly baldheaded; and at my first words seemed both angered and frightened. My obvious friendliness, however, finally melted him; and he grudgingly motioned to me to follow him up the dark, creaking and rickety attic stairs. His room, one of only two in the steeply pitched garret, was on the west side, toward the high wall that formed the upper end of the street. Its size was very great, and seemed the greater because of its extraordinary barrenness and neglect. Of furniture there was only a narrow iron bedstead, a dingy washstand, a small table, a large bookcase, an iron music-rack, and three old-fashioned chairs. Sheets of music were piled in disorder about the floor. The walls were of bare boards, and had probably never known plaster; whilst the abundance of dust and cobwebs made the place seem more deserted than inhabited. Evidently Erich Zann's world of beauty lay in some far cosmos of the imagination.

Motioning me to sit down, the dumb man closed the door, turned the large wooden bolt, and lighted a candle to augment the one he had brought with him. He now removed his viol from its moth-eaten covering, and taking it, seated himself in the least uncomfortable of the chairs. He did not employ the music-rack, but, offering no choice and playing from memory, enchanted me for over an hour with strains I had never heard before; strains which must have been of his own devising. To describe their exact nature is impossible for one unversed in music. They were a kind of fugue, with recurrent passages of the most captivating quality, but to me were notable for the absence of any of the weird notes I had overheard from my room below on other occasions.

Those haunting notes I had remembered, and had often hummed and whistled inaccurately to myself, so when the player at length laid down his bow I asked him if he would render some of them. As I began my request the wrinkled satyr-like face lost the bored placidity it had possessed during the playing, and seemed to show the same curious mixture of anger and fright which I had noticed when first I accosted the old man. For a moment I was inclined to use persuasion, regarding rather lightly the whims of senility; and even tried to awaken my host's weirder mood by whistling a few of the strains to which I had listened the night before. But I did not pursue this course for more than a moment; for when the dumb musician recognized the whistled air his face grew suddenly distorted with an expression wholly beyond analysis, and his long, cold, bony right hand reached out to stop my mouth and silence the crude imitation. As he did this he further demonstrated his eccentricity by casting a startled glance toward the lone curtained window, as if fearful of some intruder—a glance doubly absurd, since the garret stood high and inaccessible above all the adjacent roofs, this window being the only point on the steep street, as the concierge had told me, from which one could see over the wall at the summit.

The old man's glance brought Blandot's remark to my mind, and with a certain capriciousness I felt a wish to look out over the wide and dizzying panorama of moonlit roofs and city lights beyond the hilltop, which of all the dwellers in the Rue d'Auseil only this crabbed musician could see. I moved toward the window and would have drawn aside the nondescript curtains, when with a frightened rage even greater than before, the dumb lodger was upon me again; this time motioning with his head toward the door as he nervously strove to drag me thither with both hands. Now thoroughly disgusted with my host, I ordered him to release me, and told him I would go at once. His clutch relaxed, and as he saw my disgust and offense, his own anger seemed to subside. He tightened his relaxing grip, but this time in a friendly manner, forcing me into a chair; then with an appearance of wistfulness crossing to the littered table, where he wrote many words with a pencil, in the labored French of a foreigner.

The note which he finally handed me was an appeal for tolerance and forgiveness. Zann said that he was old, lonely, and afflicted with strange fears and nervous disorders connected with his music and with other things. He had enjoyed my listening to his music, and wished I would come again and not mind his eccentricities. But he could not play to another his weird harmonies, and could not bear hearing them from another; nor could he bear having anything in his room touched by another. He had not known until our hallway conversation that I could overhear his playing in my room, and now asked me if I would arrange with Blandot to take a lower room where I could not hear him in the night. He would, he wrote, defray the difference in rent.

As I sat deciphering the execrable French, I felt more lenient toward the old man. He was a victim of physical and nervous suffering, as was I; and my metaphysical studies had taught me kindness. In the silence there came a slight sound from the window—the shutter must have rattled in the night wind, and for some reason I started almost as violently as did Erich Zann. So when I had finished reading, I shook my host by the hand, and departed as a friend.

The next day Blandot gave me a more expensive room on the third floor, between the apartments of an aged money-lender and the room of a respectable upholsterer. There was no one on the fourth floor.

It was not long before I found that Zann's eagerness for my company was not as great as it had seemed while he was persuading me to move down from the fifth story. He did not ask me to call on him, and when I did call he appeared uneasy and played listlessly. This was always at night—in the day he slept and would admit no one. My liking for him did not grow, though the attic room and the weird music seemed to hold an odd fascination for me. I had a curious desire to look out of that window, over the wall and down the unseen slope at the glittering roofs and spires, which must lie outspread there. Once I went up to the garret during theater hours, when Zann was away, but the door was locked.

What I did succeed in doing was to overhear the nocturnal playing of the dumb old man. At first I would tiptoe up to my old fifth floor, then I grew bold enough to climb the last creaking staircase to the peaked garret. There in the narrow hall, outside the bolted door with the covered keyhole, I often heard sounds, which filled me with an indefinable dread—the dread of vague wonder and brooding mystery. It was not that the sounds were hideous, for they were not; but that they held vibrations suggesting nothing on this globe of earth, and that at certain intervals they assumed a symphonic quality which I could hardly conceive as produced by one player. Certainly, Erich Zann was a genius of wild power. As the weeks passed, the playing grew wilder, whilst the old musician acquired an increasing haggardness and furtiveness pitiful to behold. He now refused to admit me at any time, and shunned me whenever we met on the stairs.

Then one night as I listened at the door, I heard the shrieking viol swell into a chaotic babel of sound; a pandemonium which would have led me to doubt my own shaking sanity had there not come from behind that barred portal a piteous proof that the horror was real—the awful, inarticulate cry which only a mute can utter, and which rises only in moments of the most terrible fear or anguish. I knocked repeatedly at the door, but received no response. Afterward I waited in the black hallway, shivering with cold and fear, till I heard the poor musician's feeble effort to rise from the floor by the aid of a chair. Believing him just conscious after a fainting fit, I renewed my rapping, at the same time calling out my name reassuringly. I heard Zann stumble to the window and close both shutter and sash, then stumble to the door, which he falteringly unfastened to admit me. This time his delight at having me present was real; for his distorted face gleamed with relief while he clutched at my coat as a child clutches at its mother's skirts.

Shaking pathetically, the old man forced me into a chair whilst he sank into another, beside which his viol and bow lay carelessly on the floor. He sat for some time inactive, nodding oddly, but having a paradoxical suggestion of intense and frightened listening. Subsequently he seemed to be satisfied, and crossing to a chair by the table wrote a brief note, handed it to me, and returned to the table, where he began to write rapidly and incessantly. The note implored me in the name of mercy, and for the sake of my own curiosity, to wait where I was while he prepared a full account in German of all the marvels and terrors which beset him. I waited, and the dumb man's pencil flew.

It was perhaps an hour later, while I still waited and while the old musician's feverishly written sheets still continued to pile up, that I saw Zann start as from the hint of a horrible shock. Unmistakably he was looking at the curtained window and listening shudderingly. Then I half fancied I heard a sound myself; though it was not a horrible sound, but rather an exquisitely low and infinitely distant musical note, suggesting a player in one of the neighboring houses, or in some abode beyond the lofty wall over which I had never been able to look. Upon Zann the effect was terrible, for, dropping his pencil, suddenly he rose, seized his viol, and commenced to rend the night with the wildest playing I had ever heard from his bow save when listening at the barred door.

It would be useless to describe the playing of Erich Zann on that dreadful night. It was more horrible than anything I had ever overheard, because I could now see the expression of his face, and could realize that this time the motive was stark fear. He was trying to make a noise; to ward something off or drown something out—what, I could not imagine, awesome though I felt it must be. The playing grew fantastic, delirious, and hysterical, yet kept to the last the qualities of supreme genius, which I knew this strange old man possessed. I recognized the air—it was a wild Hungarian dance popular in the theaters, and I reflected for a moment that this was the first time I had ever heard Zann play the work of another composer.

Louder and louder, wilder and wilder, mounted the shrieking and whining of that desperate viol. The player was dripping with an uncanny perspiration and twisted like a monkey, always looking frantically at the curtained window. In his frenzied strains I could almost see shadowy satyrs and bacchanals dancing and whirling insanely through seething abysses of clouds and smoke and lightning. And then I thought I heard a shriller, steadier note that was not from the viol; a calm, deliberate, purposeful, mocking note from far away in the West.

At this juncture the shutter began to rattle in a howling night wind which had sprung up outside as if in answer to the mad playing within. Zann's screaming viol now outdid itself emitting sounds I had never thought a viol could emit. The shutter rattled more loudly, unfastened, and commenced slamming against the window. Then the glass broke shiveringly under the persistent impacts, and the chill wind rushed in, making the candles sputter and rustling the sheets of paper on the table where Zann had begun to write out his horrible secret. I looked at Zann, and saw that he was past conscious observation. His blue eyes were bulging, glassy and sightless, and the frantic playing had become a blind, mechanical, unrecognizable orgy that no pen could even suggest.

A sudden gust, stronger than the others, caught up the manuscript and bore it toward the window. I followed the flying sheets in desperation, but they were gone before I reached the demolished panes. Then I remembered my old wish to gaze from this window, the only window in the Rue d'Auseil from which one might see the slope beyond the wall, and the city outspread beneath. It was very dark, but the city's lights always burned, and I expected to see them there amidst the rain and wind. Yet when I looked from that highest of all gable windows, looked while the candles sputtered and the insane viol howled with the night-wind, I saw no city spread below, and no friendly lights gleamed from remembered streets, but only the blackness of space illimitable; unimagined space alive with motion and music, and having no semblance of anything on earth. And as I stood there looking in terror, the wind blew out both the candles in that ancient peaked garret, leaving me in savage and impenetrable darkness with chaos and pandemonium before me, and the demon madness of that night-baying viol behind me.

I staggered back in the dark, without the means of striking a light, crashing against the table, overturning a chair, and finally groping my way to the place where the blackness screamed with shocking music. To save myself and Erich Zann I could at least try, whatever the powers opposed to me. Once I thought some chill thing brushed me, and I screamed, but my scream could not be heard above that hideous viol. Suddenly out of the blackness the madly sawing bow struck me, and I knew I was close to the player. I felt ahead, touched the back of Zann's chair, and then found and shook his shoulder in an effort to bring him to his senses.

He did not respond, and still the viol shrieked on without slackening. I moved my hand to his head, whose mechanical nodding I was able to stop, and shouted in his ear that we must both flee from the unknown things of the night. But he neither answered me nor abated the frenzy of his unutterable music, while all through the garret strange currents of wind seemed to dance in the darkness and babel. When my hand touched his ear I shuddered, though I knew not why—knew not why till I felt the still face; the ice-cold, stiffened, unbreathing face whose glassy eyes bulged uselessly into the void. And then, by some miracle, finding the door and the large wooden bolt, I plunged wildly away from that glassy-eyed thing in the dark, and from the ghoulish howling of that accursed viol whose fury increased even as I plunged.

Leaping, floating, flying down those endless stairs through the dark house; racing mindlessly out into the narrow, steep, and ancient street of steps and tottering houses; clattering down steps and over cobbles to the lower streets and the putrid canyon-walled river; panting across the great dark bridge to the broader, healthier streets and boulevards we know; all these are terrible impressions that linger with me. And I recall that there was no wind, and that the moon was out, and that all the lights of the city twinkled.

Despite my most careful searches and investigations, I have never since been able to find the Rue d'Auseil. But I am not wholly sorry; either for this or for the loss in undreamable abysses of the closely-written sheets which alone could have explained the music of Erich Zann.

THE END

WIDOW HOUSE

By Gregory Luce

Sometimes old dark houses hold a lot more than ghosts—and in greater numbers, too!

Five hundred bucks a month for a furnished house was a steal, even if it *was* for the old widow Larkin's house. She had died some time back and her grandson Johnny made me a helluva deal to rent the old place. I'm sure part of it was because it had sat vacant for the better part of a year, but I think part of it was also because Johnny and I had gone to grade school together. Not that we had been close pals or anything like that. He was two years older and frankly I don't ever remember playing with him on the Sharpstein playground, but Johnny Larkin was the kind of longtime Walla Walla resident who appreciated the town he grew up in and the folks who lived there. He still lived in his childhood home just a block up Whitman Street toward Pioneer Park.

"You're a good guy, Nathan," he told me the day he handed over the key. "Take good care of the place and watch out for spiders…there's a million of 'em."

As good of a deal as it was, though, the widow Larkin's house was still basically an old, rundown piece of crap. It was one of those depressed, creaky, crumbling houses you often find single elderly people living in that they can't maintain by themselves anymore. Even when I was a kid (we had lived just a few houses up the street) the place looked dilapidated. It was a small two-story structure with an overgrown lawn, surrounded on its outer perimeter by a thick, tall green hedge that came up to eye level for most kids. There were a number of lofty, aging trees with long, gnarled branches that blocked out much of the sunlight. The cement walkway leading up to the front porch hadn't been edged in years and was partially concealed by long grass that hung over its surface. Wild bushes and broken, twisted trellises jealously hugged the outside walls. When I was a kid we used to sneak into the sagging garage on the back of the property and one time I broke through the rotting floorboards of the upper loft. I caught myself with my arms as I was falling through, otherwise it would have been a sure trip to the hospital in the back of Mom's green '59 Fairlane.

Although I lived in Walla Walla for many years as a youth, I had never actually seen the inside of the place until the day Johnny showed me around. It wasn't in any better shape than the outside. Everything was ancient: the drapes, the carpet, the furniture, even the paint on the walls. A door in the kitchen led down to a musty, unfinished basement with a prehistoric furnace that belched out thick, oppressive heat. It was dark and even a little scary down there so I stayed out of it as much as possible. The widow Larkin had passed away nearly a year before, yet the house still smelled like an old person. The air was heavy and carried a hint of decay. After I moved in I kept the doors and windows open constantly until the late autumn weather forced me to keep them closed.

"It's not much to look at but its livable," Johnny told me the day after I moved in. I wrote down a few things that needed fixing around the house, the worst of which was a broken toilet in one of the bathrooms. Johnny had a reputation for being cheap and he grimaced when I handed him the list.

Yet in spite of all its faults, the late widow Larkin's house was a welcome refuge from some of the harsher realities of life that had nearly smothered me in recent times. It started with the untimely death of my beloved Julie (a long battle with kidney disease) and was followed by a string of financial setbacks that left me virtually destitute. After living with friends for several months I was grateful to secure a fulltime job as an assistant librarian over at Marcus College. The position wasn't all that much, but the benefits were decent and the salary was enough to pay for food, rent, and even an occasional gallon of gas. I did some part time writing on the side that occasionally brought in some extra dollars. All I wanted was to settle in somewhere and escape from life's troubles for a while, maybe a glass of wine or two in the evenings set to a Brahms symphony.

It was early that fall when I met my neighbor, Ashley Barnes. She lived in the dark green duplex across the street. Sometimes I'd see her walking her Schnauzer up and down Whitman. She'd wave whenever she saw me. It always made me chuckle because there was a little doggie poop bag in her hand that swung back and forth as she waved. She knocked on my door one day a few weeks after I moved in. I offered her a glass of wine and asked her to come in and visit for awhile.

"I'm a food service administrator over at Walla Walla General Hospital," she told me.

She was a nice, fairly good-looking gal in her mid-forties with no kids; I suppose I might have been interested had I not still been grieving over Julie. She sat on my couch telling me all about the virtues of hospital food, but just the presence of another woman sometimes brought back my sadness about Julie and at that moment it was drowning out all of Ashley's conversation.

Julie…Julie…why did you have to leave? I miss you so much.

Ashley proved to be a good neighbor, though, often stopping by to say hello or see how I was doing—a real sweet lady. However, as happy as she always seemed, I think there was a bit of loneliness hiding somewhere behind that adorable smile of hers. I finally succumbed to her small town charms and asked her out to lunch one Saturday. After that we began seeing each other on a fairly regular basis. We started with a few dinner and movie dates, but I never let it go much beyond that, though she did tongue me a little one night when I kissed her good night. I knew there might be something more than friendship heating up so I decided to move along very cautiously.

It was in late October that I first saw the black widow. It was sitting right in the middle of the kitchen windowsill. It was the biggest, fattest, scariest damned black widow I had ever seen in my life. I must have stood and stared at it for a good 30 seconds. I darted into the dining room and grabbed a magazine so I could smash the tiny monster before it got away. When I returned a few seconds later, though, it was gone. I looked all over the kitchen, but it had vanished without a trace—probably through some crack in the kitchen wall. I told Ashley about the black widow over dinner the next evening.

"There are tons of black widows in our neighborhood," she told me. "You should get Larkin to fumigate the place."

"Fat chance of that happening," I responded, remembering Johnny's hesitancy toward fixing other things around the house.

"Seriously, Nathan, old Mr. Beckman died of multiple bites just a few months ago."

"Who's old Mr. Beckman?"

"He lived three doors up Whitman from your place. You know…the house with all the Raspberry vines in the back. They brought him into General late one morning. He was bitten during the night. It was awful. It's hard to save a 90-year-old man who had as many widow bites as he did."

One evening later that week I saw the black widow again, this time on the fireplace mantle. I was sure it was the same one because of its size. I was lying on the couch reading Tolkein for the umpteenth time when I saw something moving out of the corner of my eye. When I looked up I saw the widow scamper down the entire length of the mantle. Before I could rise it disappeared through a hole between the fireplace bricks. Then something unusual happened. As I lay on the couch I could hear faint laughing coming from somewhere within the house. It was a soft female laugh, nothing that unusual in nature, just a gentle laugh like your mom or grandmother would have made at something cute you did when you were five years old. I rose off the couch and casually looked about the house but found nothing. I shrugged it off and chalked it up to an active imagination.

I found three more widows the very next day, all down in that dank, musty basement. None of them, however, were my fat friend from the night before. One was nestled in the corner of a small upper basement window, two others were in the rafters. I nailed them all with bug spray; then I went over the whole room for good measure, spraying indiscriminately in every direction. On the far wall right across from the old furnace I noticed something odd. There was a gaping crack in the cement. It was jagged in nature and several inches across at its widest point. It started right at the base of the wall and crawled up the cold cement for a couple of feet. I pointed my flashlight into it.

"We'll I'll be…" I whispered with surprise.

I was startled to find that the crack went all the way through the basement wall. It was really more of a jagged hole than anything else. Furthermore, there appeared to be a very small tunnel extending right into the earth beyond. I figured it was an abandoned rodent tract of some sort, a gopher…maybe a mole. I needed to tell Larkin about this, some cement patchwork would have to be done. Just to be on the safe side I sprinkled some rodent poison on the basement floor in front of it.

That night I dreamed about Julie. I tossed and turned all night long.

Over the next few days I saw an increasing number of not only black widows, but other spiders as well. I kept my bug spray handy and doused them generously whenever I saw them. I concluded the increasing coolness of the autumn weather was bringing them inside. Ashley's advice from weeks before came back to me and I thought seriously of calling an exterminator. One Sunday afternoon I walked into the living room to see the big black widow sitting up on the fireplace mantle again. It was the first time I had seen the fat little beast in some time.

"Well hi there, sweetie," I spoke softly.

I don't know if it was all in my mind, but I could swear it stared right back at me as though completely unafraid, as though it was sizing me up for something awful. I found this a little unnerving. Not wanting to startle it, I moved slowly toward the kitchen where I had left the bug spray sitting next to the basement door. I hadn't taken two steps, though, before it disappeared into the same hole it had escaped through before. I was startled by how fast it moved.

Later that afternoon I switched on the TV. *Tarantula* with John Agar was playing on an oldies cable network. I tuned in right as the giant spider was crawling out of a flaming laboratory. I telephoned Ashley and begged her to come over and keep me company. We watched the rest of the movie over a plate of cheese and a bottle of Merlot. Afterward I told her about the black widows and my thoughts of calling a pest control company.

"Larkin is really the guy who should be calling the exterminator, Nathan. Not you."

I almost choked. "Johnny Larkin's a nice guy, but he's a cheap SOB, too. I can't even get him to fix a hole in my basement wall or the toilet in the hallway bathroom."

"Well…it's a smart thing for you to get done…regardless of who pays. A house in this part of town can get overrun with the little monsters if you don't keep them contained."

That night I drank a Brandy and went to sleep listening to a new recording of Debussy's nocturnes. Later on I dreamed of Julie again, part of it was sweet, part of it was bitter. I woke up with a start around 4:00am and couldn't get back to sleep. As I lay waiting for the dawn I suddenly heard the same soft laughing that I had heard a few weeks earlier. It seemed to be coming again from somewhere in the house. But this time it was different.

This time it made my flesh creep.

As before, the timbre of the laugh seemed innocent in nature, but contrasted against the darkness of the room and the stillness of the hour it suddenly took on a perverse quality that I hadn't noticed previously. Its innocuous tone struck me as a façade for something loathsome, as if something vile was hiding beneath the surface. I sat up in bed and listened more intently. It continued faintly for a few moments, then faded into the stillness. In the living room I heard the Regulator strike 5:00am. I got up and threw my robe and slippers on. This time I searched the entire house thoroughly, but there was still no one to be found. When I finally settled back into bed I couldn't help feeling a little spooked. What had I heard? Could there really have been an unknown woman in my house at five o'clock in the morning?

"Preposterous," I mumbled, then rolled over.

It must have been something else, I reasoned, perhaps the cooing of a night bird or the early morning chattering of a squirrel somewhere outside my bedroom window or up on the roof. I didn't fall back to sleep until shortly before my alarm sounded.

Over the next few days it started getting cold. An Indian summer had graced us with good weather for many weeks, but now the early stages of winter were starting to set in. I hadn't used the furnace much because I hated the old beast. It looked to be right out of the 1930s, complete with what I assumed to be asbestos siding. The air that pumped out of it was most oppressive and carried a slight odor of something foul, even making me a little dizzy at times. I don't know what kind of mechanism was inside it, but the whole house would shake whenever it fired up—literally shake like a sudden earth tremor had hit. One time a drinking glass, sitting on the edge of the bathroom sink, fell to the floor and shattered. On another occasion a can of Dennison's Chili Con Carne with no beans had vibrated off the kitchen counter and nearly landed on my foot. Not only that, but on more than one occasion the hallway thermostat hadn't worked properly and the house ended up getting unbearably hot. One frosty night I woke up drenched in sweat. The thermostat was set for 68 degrees, but the temperature in the house was 91 and the relentless contraption below was still belching out hot air. I fiddled with the thermostat for several minutes before the furnace finally lumbered to a halt. Since that night I had only used the fireplace, but with the colder weather coming on I knew I would have go back to the furnace again, sooner or later. Sure enough, later that week the thermostat went crazy again. I woke up after midnight and found the temperature even hotter than before. I called Johnny about it the next morning. He assured me a repairman would come out the following week.

That Saturday I spent much of the morning going through unpacked boxes that had been sitting around since the day I moved in. They were piled up high in the widow Larkin's former bedroom. I had decided early on against using her old room as my master bedroom. Her death had been quite sudden, coming in the middle of the night from a massive heart attack, so there was something a little too creepy about sleeping in the bed that an old lady had croaked in. I took the bedroom across the hall instead.

I worked for about an hour unpacking things and finding places for them around the house. I was hanging some seldom-used clothes in the widow Larkin's old closet when I noticed something on the upper shelf. I reached up and pulled down a peculiar-looking apparatus. It appeared to be some kind of small cage. Its top, bottom, and sides were made out of window screen that was locked into place by a wooden, skeletal frame. The whole thing was rectangular-shaped, probably a foot in length and about four inches in width and height. On top there was a small square-shaped portal protruding upward a couple of inches. At the top of that was a little trapdoor with a tiny latch. I couldn't be sure, but the entire unit appeared to have been made by hand. As I held it up I gasped with surprise. Inside the cage were the crumbling remains of numerous insects: flies, moths, crickets—there was even the shell of a good-sized beetle. The device looked like it was somebody's idea of a miniature torture dungeon. The insect remains crumbled into dust when I shook them out into the bathroom sink. Then I noticed something curious. At one end there was a small hole in the corner of the screen. It protruded outward, as though something had pushed through from inside, as though something had escaped from its cage. I called up Ashley and told her about my unusual find.

"This is one of the oddest things I've ever seen," I told her. "Looks like the widow Larkin had a penchant for imprisoning bugs. Wait'll you see it"

Ashley sounded repulsed. "Boy oh boy, I can hardly wait."

Late that afternoon brought me out to the old garage that sat on the back of the property next to an alley that ran through the middle of the block. I always parked my car on the street and I hadn't been in the garage more than a few times. There had been some bad wind gusts the night before and the front porch was covered in leaves, so I was hoping to find a big push broom. I slid the long, creaky wooden door open and immediately noticed a rancid odor. It took a moment for my eyes to adjust to the dimness inside, then I saw something grim in the far corner.

It was a dead cat.

At least I thought it was a dead cat. The body looked like a cat, but it was hard to say at first glance because the face of the creature, especially the nose, was so bloated that the usual feline features were distorted into something obscenely grotesque. I tried to move in for a closer look but the smell was putrid and it nearly made me sick. I was forced to retreat into the house. Inside I gave Ashley a quick call.

"Can you come over? I found something pretty awful in my garage."

"I'll be there in a minute," she told me.

After we hung up I returned to the garage brandishing a flashlight and holding a hand towel over my face. Bending down over the dead animal I focused the light on its head. It was a cat all right, dead for at least a few days, maybe a week. I was surprised I hadn't noticed the smell before. Its nose and face were a puffy mess. I glanced around when I heard Ashley's footsteps approaching.

"Grab a towel from under the kitchen sink and put it over your face. It smells bloody awful out here."

She returned a few moments later holding a pink wash cloth over her nose. She bent down next to me and examined the dead creature, poking it and rolling it over with a stick. Maggots crawled out of its rotting flesh.

"Looks like the poor thing was poisoned," she told me. "If I didn't know better I'd swear some kind of snake must have bit it right on the nose. Look how bloated the bridge of its nose is."

She jabbed the stick directly into the swollen tissue.

"Couldn't be a snake, though," she said. "You never find poisonous snakes in the city."

"How about a spider?" I asked.

Ashley shot me a curious glance, then looked at me thoughtfully. "The only place a cat could conceivably be bitten by a spider is right on the nose. The skin on the footpads is too thick and the fur's too deep everywhere else...and the cat would almost certainly have to be asleep in order for that to happen."

"Bitten right on the end of its nose by a black widow spider while it was curled up asleep," I suggested.

A spooky expression came over Ashley's face. She started shaking her head from side to side. "I don't know, Nate. This whole black widow thing is getting a little bizarre. Have you called Larkin about an exterminator yet?"

"First thing Monday morning," I answered. "That's a promise."

That night I dreamed about spiders—lots and lots of spiders.

I called Johnny about an exterminator Monday morning. He tried to tell me my spider problem was nothing to worry about.

"Just leave 'em alone and they won't bother you. My grandma lived in that house for years and they never bothered her, in fact I think she used to kinda' like 'em." He chuckled reflectively. "I've got to admit, my granny was kind of a weird old broad."

"What do you mean?"

"Oh…I dunno…she just had a lot of different interests. She kept pretty much to herself the last years of her life. I remember she used to catch crickets and other bugs and throw them into the spider webs around her garden. She told me it helped keep the insect population down…which I guess is true…but it always struck me that she kinda' enjoyed doing it. Sometimes she would laugh when she was dropping them into the webs…nothing sinister…just a cute little old lady 'happy' laugh." Larkin chuckled. "Like I said…my granny was a weird old broad."

Johnny assured me that if the problem worsened he would have an exterminator come out and give the place a good dousing. "Just give it to the end of the first big cold snap and most of them will probably be gone. There's no food supply for 'em this time of the year."

The second Friday of December was the start of an eventful weekend. I left campus and came over to the house during lunch to let Larkin's repairman in to look at the thermostat. I expected some crusty old Walla Walla regular in dirty coveralls and a Walla Walla Grain Growers cap, but what I got was a talkative young woman with an Annie Lennox haircut in a Led Zeppelin tee-shirt and jeans. She carried an oversized toolbox and a laptop computer. Her shirt was cut off around the bottom and her midriff exposed the colorful tattoo of a coiled cobra.

"What's the computer for?" I asked.

"For researching furnace types and checking parts inventories," she replied. "What kind of trouble have you been having?"

"Thermostat's busted," I answered. I showed her the hallway thermostat and gave her a rundown on my overheating problems. She fiddled with the thermostat for a couple of minutes.

"It might not actually be the thermostat," she told me. "Could be a furnace problem. Where is it?"

"Down in the basement." I gave her a big smile. "And it's one of those antediluvian monoliths." I pointed toward the kitchen. "Let me show you where it's at, then I gotta get back to work. After you're done, just let yourself out and make sure the door's locked behind you. Be sure to send Larkin the bill."

"Sure enough," she replied.

I moved into the kitchen, opened the basement door, and flipped on the switch. The basement below filled with pale yellow light

"Have fun," I kidded her.

Toolbox in hand, she disappeared below. A few moments later I was on my way back to work.

I got off about 3:00pm that afternoon. Molly Duncan, my boss and head librarian who was a single 51-year-old woman in the middle of a mid-life crisis with a penchant for 25-year old bachelors, often let us go a little early on Fridays, which was always nice. However, I suspect it wasn't so much because she wanted us to have a good weekend as much as she wanted to leave early herself, which she often did, leaving the library in the hands of student aides until closing time.

"Go out and get a good start on the weekend," she would tell us with a big, insincere smile on her face.

When I got back to the house I found things rather odd. The front door to the house was slightly ajar. Inside I found a wrench and a pair of pliers lying in the middle of the living room. As I stepped across the room I saw a screwdriver lying near the kitchen entryway. The repair lady's laptop computer was on the kitchen counter, exactly where she had left it earlier in the day. The basement door was wide open and the light was still on downstairs.

I called softly into the dimness below, "Hello…anybody down there?"

There was no response. The silence left me ill at ease. I could see another wrench hanging precariously off one of the steps. I slowly descended down the stairs and looked around. The repair lady was nowhere in sight. I came around near the furnace. There was another screwdriver sitting on the floor and there were several screws lying near it. They appeared to have been unscrewed from a metal plate that ran across the bottom front of the furnace. I couldn't tell for sure, but other than the screws lying on the floor it appeared the furnace hadn't been tampered with at all, let alone repaired. I screwed the loose screws back into the furnace.

"Strange…" I muttered under my breath. I suddenly had a mental image of the repair lady running up the stairs and out of the house as fast as she could, tools bouncing out of her toolbox along the way. If that was indeed what had happened it certainly helped make sense out of all the tools that were strewn about, but why she might have left in such a hurry was a mystery. I flipped open my cell phone and called Larkin.

"Looks like the furnace repair lady may have left in an awful big hurry…there's a trail of tools from the basement all the way to the front door. To tell you the truth, I don't think she even did any repairs. Something must have happened. She even left her laptop sitting on the kitchen counter."

Johnny was surprised. "That's damn peculiar, Nathan. Let me call the furnace company and find out what's going on. I'll call you back in a few minutes."

I walked about the house and picked up the scattered tools. I found another screwdriver lying near the front door and a small penlight on the walkway outside. A couple of minutes later the phone rang. It was Larkin.

"I just spoke to the service manager. The girl called him about an hour ago…said she was taken sick and had to go home."

"You're kidding. She looked okay to me. When I left the house to go back to work she seemed fine."

"I dunno…that's what he told me. It's funny, though…he said that when she called in she sounded kinda' strange…said her voice sounded kinda'…trembly. She even asked him to call you and see if you'd return the company's laptop for her."

"She wants *me* to return it?

"Yeah…he said something about her not wanting to come back over to the house…something about her not knowing anything about your kind of furnace. Sounded like phony baloney to me, but I wasn't gonna call his repair girl a liar. Don't worry about it, though. The guy told me he'd have another repairman out first thing Monday morning. They can pick it up then."

I got off the phone, but an uneasy feeling remained and I was troubled by it. Something out of the norm had happened with the repair lady and I sensed I wasn't getting the whole story. Whether the service manager was holding back something from Johnny and me I didn't know. Perhaps the repair lady was holding back something from him. Whatever the case, I had an intuitive feeling that something was amiss.

That evening Ashley and I bundled up and took a long walk through Pioneer Park in the cold. The park was enveloped in darkness and quiet, but its tranquility was soothing. It had been a long week. I put my arm around Ashley as we strolled.

"Did I tell you I landed a writing job?" I asked her as we passed under a giant Sycamore tree.

"No you didn't." She tugged at my arm. "So tell me about it."

"The Bulletin wants me to write a series of articles on unusual local businesses. You know…antique shops, galleries, eclectic restaurants…that kind of thing. The first article's due Sunday morning. Ten articles over ten weeks. They're going to be running them in the Potpourri section on Mondays. In fact…I really should be home writing right now."

Ashley got a pleading look on her face and tugged at my arm again. "Do it tomorrow…please?"

We returned to her apartment and gobbled down some carryout Chinese food we picked up on the way home. Gorging myself with General Tsao chicken never seemed so pleasurable as with Ashley Barnes sitting across the table from me. She seemed more beautiful each time I saw her. We settled in and watched an old Bette Davis movie from the 1940s that made her cry. Tears streamed down her cheeks. I wrapped my arm around her and she leaned into my shoulder.

A sea of sorrow and self-pity can only last so long before you either break free or its misery drags you down completely. The chains around my heart unshackled that evening. Ashley and I ended up spending the night together at her apartment. I wasn't looking for it to happen but it just did, and it felt good—no guilt, no remorse. I would always love Julie, but I knew in my heart she would be happy if I found someone else and moved on. The next morning Ashley and I went out for breakfast at the campus coffee shop.

She looked at me tentatively. "So…is last night going to send you running for the hills?" Her expression made it clear she was a little fearful of my answer.

I smiled warmly at her. "I think I'll stick around for awhile."

She reached across the table and grasped my hand. We spent the next several hours together before I returned home to work on my writing assignment.

"I'll be over later tonight…after the article's done."

She smiled and spoke softly to me. "I'll wait up for you."

Late that afternoon gave us the first heavy snowfall of the year—six inches by 7:00pm. There were cars sliding into the curb all up and down Whitman Street. By mid-evening the skies cleared, though, and the temperature dropped into the mid-twenties. It was getting damned cold so I turned up the thermostat. I sat in front of the computer working on the article, the furnace pumping its hot, nasty air throughout the house. It was difficult to concentrate and the smell of the furnace seemed more pungent than usual. The phone rang—it was Ashley.

"How's it going?"

"Got about another hour. Gettin' sleepy, though. I'll be over as soon as I'm done."

After we got off the phone I popped open a wine cooler and dropped a disc into the CD player: *Rachmaninoff Piano Concertos Nos. 1 and 4.* My favorite classical pieces always helped me concentrate. I labored on into the evening as Philippe Entremont's magical fingers rolled up and down the keyboard with Ormandy and the Philadelphia Orchestra in accompaniment. But still I felt drowsiness setting in. My head bobbed up and down like I was fighting sleep behind the wheel at the end of a long road trip. If I could close my eyes for just a few minutes, that's all I needed. It was getting hot in the room; the air in the house seemed stifling.

Gawd…that furnace stinks tonight.

My eyelids seemed heavier and heavier by the minute. I couldn't keep them open much longer. I felt a little dizzy. Just a few minutes rest, that's all. I laid my head down next to the keyboard. My mind wandered off into la-la land. I had images of Ashley. Sweet images. They were interrupted by a blurred stabbing sensation. But my exhaustion was too strong. I slipped away.

A short while later I was awakened by Sergei Rachmaninoff. A sudden orchestral crescendo at the beginning of the final movement of his fourth piano concerto brought me back to semi-consciousness. I had been asleep for about half an hour.

And I felt terrible.

I raised my head up and opened my eyes. Everything seemed a little blurred. I looked down at myself and realized that I was soaked in perspiration. My breathing felt heavy and the heat was almost suffocating. I stood up, but as I rose I felt my abdominal muscles cramp. There was a mild feeling of nausea and my sense of consciousness was different…dizzy…almost as though I was in the middle of a dream.

"All right…what in the world is going on here?" I muttered to myself.

I sat back down for a minute and shook my head, trying to clear the cobwebs. The room was still filled with music.

Entrement's fingers were running up and down the keyboard in a series of dazzling arpeggios and glissandos. But the normally romantic strains of Rachmaninoff's music now sounded different, almost as though a sorcerer was sitting at the keyboard spinning some uncanny musical tale. I rose up again and moved unsteadily down the hallway to check the thermostat. Sure enough, the furnace had gone screwy again. The temperature was 93 degrees. I fiddled with the damned thing for a minute, cursing below my breath, but the stream of hot air blasting from below continued unabated. A hot stench wafted through every room in the house.

I stumbled into the kitchen. The sensation of dizziness and nausea was getting more pronounced. My throat seemed tight and it was becoming hard to breathe normally. I was sure there must be something wrong with the air coming out of the vents. That had to be it. I opened the basement door and flipped the switch. The light below seemed dimmer than usual. I lumbered carefully down the stairs and over to the furnace. I was surprised to find it even hotter in the basement. Perspiration was beading up on my forehead and running into my eyes, stinging them and causing my vision to blur with its salty content.

I had never really looked that closely at the furnace before. Perhaps there was a manual switch I could use to shut it down. Then, for the first time since I had awakened, I noticed the pain on top of my left hand. With everything else that was going on with me physically I hadn't noticed it until that moment, but the tissue seemed to be throbbing. I held it up close to the yellow bulb overhead and was shocked to see it was puffy and swollen. Even in the weak light I could see a tiny puncture at the very top of the swollen mass. I shuddered.

I knew it was a spider bite.

Then the furnace abruptly stopped. The only sounds in the house now were the muffled strains of Rachmaninoff's wild music filtering down from the bedroom above. At that moment I saw something moving out of the corner of my eye in the gloom beyond the furnace. I looked over and squinted at the far wall. The cement surface around the big hole appeared to be alive with movement. I leaned in a step or two to get a closer look. The next moment I recoiled in horror. I was thunderstruck to see a wave of black widow spiders spewing out of the jagged crack. The wall and floor around the hole were crawling with them. With as much speed as I could muster, I staggered upstairs and slammed the door behind me.

Then I saw the can of bug spray sitting on the kitchen counter.

For a brief moment I entertained the thought of returning below and killing the little bastards. I picked up the can and reached for the doorknob. Then I came to my senses. *What the hell do you think you're doing, Nathan?* There were far too many of them to fight with a single can of bug spray. Besides, I was feeling even dizzier than before. My stomach was hurting and I thought I might throw up. The room began spinning and I started to totter. I sat the can of bug spray on the edge of the kitchen table and moved toward the living room. I needed to get outside into the fresh air. I crossed the threshold and staggered. I was reeling from the venom that circulated through my veins. My legs started to give way. I spun around and collapsed on the living room carpet—flat on my face in front of the kitchen entryway.

Everything became fuzzy at this point. I reached my hands out to try and push myself up but I was too weak. I needed to lay there for a moment and regain my strength. I closed my eyes for a few seconds. The Rachmaninoff concerto that was echoing throughout the house abruptly climaxed in an agitated crescendo of piano and orchestral wizardry. The house was suddenly dead quiet. Then through the silence I heard a most terrifying thing. From somewhere behind the basement door I could hear the faint tittering of an old woman, laughing softly at my horrible predicament.

Then I felt something on my right hand—something prickly—*something moving.*

I raised my head to see the fat black widow sitting on top of my hand. It was staring at me, sizing me up as it had done weeks before. Before I could begin to react it sunk its fangs down into my skin. The pain was sharp—and searing. I gurgled in horror and tried to slap it away with my other hand, which was already swollen with its venom. I was far too groggy, though, and the widow too fast. I swung feebly and missed it completely. The widow dashed through the entryway onto the kitchen floor.

Then, as if by the grace of God, the furnace fired up again. For an instant the whole house shook. In my earlier moment of dizziness I had set the can of bug spray on the edge of the kitchen table—right on the very edge, even hanging out a little I think. The sudden vibration sent it tumbling to the floor below. When it hit the grimy linoleum surface it commenced to roll. The widow, which was scampering toward the basement door, literally jumped in the air when the giant canister crashed an inch or two away and began to roll toward it. This can of bug spray was a big one (Black Flag Home and Garden) and practically full. Before the fat monster could even react, the can rolled over it, crushing part of its abdomen and several of its legs. But the widow was only injured, not flattened. It limped along in a total panic now, a slow, jittery crawl toward the perceived safety of the basement below.

With the greatest of effort, perhaps fueled by a craving for revenge, I rose up from the floor and hovered over the retreating arachnoid. I was still reeling with the effects of its venom so I braced myself against the wall next to the basement door. I looked down and lifted my right foot a few inches off the floor.

"Goodbye, sweetie."

My foot smashed down and squashed the black widow's guts into a slimy mess. Crushing a bug had never felt so good in my life. The crunching of its body vibrated up my leg like a deep massage, easing the pain, dizziness, and nausea of two black widow bites. At that moment I actually managed to smile. A big smile, too—ear to ear.

However, my elation only lasted for a moment. From beyond the basement door on the stairwell below came an almost imperceptible sound. It was the collective scream of a thousand tiny voices crying out in hateful rage. Seconds later a torrent of black widows began pouring out from under the basement door onto the linoleum floor. My feeling of euphoria turned to a rush of unmitigated terror as I wheeled around and stumbled out of the kitchen. As I stepped into the living room I briefly turned and looked back toward the kitchen entryway:

Hundreds of black widows were dancing across the linoleum and onto the carpet behind me.

I gasped and pitched forward toward the front door. When I swung the door open, the blast of frigid winter air almost knocked me over. I staggered out into the snow. I managed to make it across Whitman and onto the parking strip in front of Ashley's duplex before the symptoms of two matching black widow bites caused me to collapse in the snow. I rolled over on my back. The stars above were icy cold.

I commenced to calling out Ashley's name, over and over.

Tuesday morning gave me my first real conversation with Ashley since I was rushed to Walla Walla General Saturday night. She had vigilantly stayed at my bedside most of Sunday, but I was so groggy I barely remembered anything at all. They stuck me with a lot of needles, too, and my conscious moments were a long painful blur. I spent most of that day sleeping. I hadn't seen Ashley at all on Monday except for a quick visit in the morning, so I was anxious to talk with her.

"Where were you yesterday?" I asked.

"Busy," she told me.

"How sick was I?"

"You went into anaphylactic shock."

"The doctor said something to me about that yesterday. I was too sleepy to care. What exactly does it mean?"

"Well, in addition to the normal effects that a black widow's venom would have on a person, it means you're also allergic to it, the same way some people are allergic to bee venom." She stroked her hand softly over my hair. "We might have lost you, Nate. We would have, too…if I hadn't heard you calling my name from outside. Lucky for you it was a somewhat mild case. Having two separate widow bites certainly didn't help things, though."

I looked at her earnestly. "Did you go into my house that night after you found me?"

She shook her head. "I was too busy dragging you out of the snow and calling 911…but I did go over Sunday morning after spending the night with you here at the hospital." Her voice lowered and she leaned closer to me. "There were black widows all over the place. *All*…over the place. On the walls…on the floors…on the ceiling…the kitchen was covered with them. There were even the bodies of a few of them trailing out onto the walkway, frozen in the snow. I got out of there in a hurry. Larkin brought in the exterminators Sunday afternoon." She smiled for a moment. "He had to pay extra for it, too." Her expression turned serious again. "They said they'd never seen anything like it, Nate. They killed a million of 'em. The only thing they could figure was that large numbers of them had somehow been attracted by the excessive heat from your furnace." She shrugged her shoulders. "I don't think they really had a clue. I gotta tell you, though, when I walked into your house Sunday morning the furnace was on full blast and the temperature must have been over a hundred degrees. I couldn't believe how hot it was in that old house."

I shook my head. "It wasn't the heat that brought those spiders in. Believe me…it wasn't the heat." I gave Ashley a full account of the frightening events of Saturday night and all the other strange occurrences from previous days. "I've never been so scared in all my life as when I heard that laughter coming up from behind the basement door." I stared out the window in the general direction of Whitman Street. "There's something in that house, Ashley. I don't know what it is…but there's something *in* that house."

Ashley didn't say anything for a moment. She got a blank expression on her face like she was trying to take it all in, trying to digest the unbelievable tale I had just told her. Then she spoke to me.

"Well, whatever it was, at least you're out of there now."

Her statement startled me a little. "What do you mean?"

"You're out of there…completely. I arranged it with Larkin. In fact he's got a 'for sale' sign in front of the place now."

"What about my things, my books, my belongings?"

"Don't worry Nathan. That's what I was doing yesterday. I had all your stuff moved into my apartment…" she paused and looked hopefully into my eyes, "…our apartment."

"*Our* apartment?"

"You need someplace to stay and you sure can't go back into that house again."

I just looked at her, a weak expression of puzzlement on my face.

"Relax, Nathan," she said almost whispering, "I'm not going to force anything on you that you're not ready for. But you need someplace to live and my rent's already paid up…two months in advance. Try it for a few weeks, and if you don't—"

I cut her off in mid-sentence as I brought my index finger up to her lips in a gesture for silence. I lowered my hand and smiled weakly at her. Her eyes twinkled, and a moment later a warm smile of affection graced her beautiful face. I reached over for her hand, closing my eyes as our fingers quietly embraced. It was going to be a long winter, and I needed a good rest.

THE END

THE DWARF

By Ray Bradbury

Bradbury's brand of magic is hard to classify. As was Charles Dickens, he is a writer of great heart. But there is much more. Instinctively a humanist, he seeks out his characters in strange byways and strives for an understanding of their needs. He respects the clown and the statesman alike, and writes of both with sympathy. His DWARF is a fine story and also, a clear plea for compassion.

AIMEE watched the sky, quietly. Tonight was one of those motionless hot summer nights. The concrete pier empty, the strung red, white, yellow bulbs burning like insects in the air above the wooden emptiness. The managers of the various carnival pitches stood, like melting wax dummies, eyes staring blindly, not talking, all down the line.

Two customers had passed through an hour before. Those two lonely people were now in the roller coaster, screaming murderously as it plummeted down the blazing night, around one emptiness after another.

Aimee moved slowly across the strand, a few worn wooden hoopla rings sticking to her wet hands. She stopped behind the ticket booth that fronted the MIRROR MAZE. She saw herself grossly misrepresented in three rippled mirrors outside the Maze. A thousand tired replicas of herself dissolved in the corridor beyond, hot images among so much clear coolness.

She stepped inside the ticket booth and stood looking a long while at Ralph Banghart's thin neck. He clenched an unlit cigar between his long uneven yellow teeth as he laid out a battered game of solitaire on the ticket shelf.

When the roller-coaster wailed and fell in its terrible avalanche again, she was reminded to speak.

"What kind of people go up in roller coasters?"

Ralph Banghart worked his cigar a full thirty seconds. "People wanna die. That rollie-coaster's the handiest thing to dying there is." He sat listening to the faint sound of rifle shots from the shooting gallery. "This whole damn carny business's crazy. For instance, that Dwarf. You *seen* him? Every night, pays his dime, runs in the Mirror Maze all the way back through to Screwy Louie's Room. You should *see* this little runt head back there. My God!"

THE
DWARF

Illustrated by Sanford Kossin

Bradbury's brand of magic is hard to classify. As was Charles Dickens, he is a writer of great heart. But there is much more. Instinctively a humanist, he seeks out his characters in strange byways and strives for an understanding of their needs. He respects the clown and the statesman alike, and writes of both with sympathy. His DWARF is a fine story and also, a clear plea for compassion.

"Oh, yes," said Aimee, remembering. "I always wonder what it's like to be a dwarf. I always feel sorry when I see him."

"I could play him like an accordion."

"Don't *say* that!"

"My Lord." Ralph patted her thigh with a free hand. "The way you carry on about guys you never even met." He shook his head and chuckled. "Him and his secret. Only he don't know *I* know, see? Boy howdy!"

"It's a hot night." She twitched the large wooden hoops nervously in her damp fingers.

"Don't change the subject. He'll be here, rain or shine."

Aimee shifted her weight. Ralph seized her elbow. "Hey! You ain't mad? You wanna see that Dwarf, don't you? Sh!" Ralph turned. "Here he comes now!"

The Dwarf's hand, hairy and dark, appeared all by itself reaching up into the booth window with a silver dime. An invisible person called, "One!" in a high child's voice.

Involuntarily, Aimee bent forward.

The Dwarf looked up at her, resembling nothing more than a dark-eyed, dark-haired, ugly man who has been locked in a wine-press, squeezed and wadded down and down, fold on fold, agony on agony, until a bleached, outraged mass is left, the face bloated shapelessly, a face you knew must stare wide-eyed and awake at two and three and four o'clock in the morning, lying flat in bed, only the body asleep.

Ralph tore a yellow ticket in half. "One!"

The Dwarf, as if frightened by an approaching storm, pulled his black coat-lapels tightly about his throat and waddled swiftly. A moment later, ten thousand lost and wandering dwarfs wriggled between the mirror flats, like frantic dark beetles, and vanished.

"Quick!"

Ralph squeezed Aimee along a dark passage behind the mirrors. She felt him pat her all the way back through the tunnel to a thin partition with a peekhole.

"This is rich," he chuckled. "Go on—look."

Aimee hesitated, then put her face to the partition.

"You *see* him?" Ralph whispered.

Aimee felt her heart beating. A full minute passed.

There stood the Dwarf in the middle of the small blue room. His eyes were shut. He wasn't ready to open them yet. Now, now he opened his eyelids and looked at a large mirror set before him. And what he saw in the mirror made him smile.

He winked, he pirouetted, he stood sidewise, he waved, he bowed, he did a little clumsy dance.

And the mirror repeated each motion with long, thin arms, with a tall, tall body, with a huge wink and an enormous repetition of the dance, ending in a *gigantic* bow!

"Every night the same thing," whispered Ralph in Aimee's ear. "Ain't that rich?"

Aimee turned her head and looked at Ralph steadily out of her motionless face for a long time, and she said nothing. Then, as if she could not help herself, she moved her head slowly and very slowly back to stare once more through the opening. She held her breath. She felt her eyes begin to water.

Ralph nudged her, whispering, "Hey, what's the little gink doin' *now?*"

They were drinking coffee and not looking at each other in the ticket booth half an hour later, when the Dwarf came out of the mirrors. He took his hat off and started to approach the booth when he saw Aimee, and hurried away.

"He wanted something," said Aimee.

"Yeah." Ralph squashed out his cigarette, idly. "I know *what,* too. But he hasn't got the nerve to ask. One night in this squeaky little voice he says, 'I bet those mirrors are expensive.' Well, I played dumb. I said yeah they were. He sort of looked at me, waiting, and when I didn't say any more, he went home, but next night he said, 'I bet those mirrors cost fifty, a hundred bucks.' I bet they do, I said. I laid me out a hand of solitaire."

"Ralph," she said.

He glanced up. "Why you *look* at me that way?"

"Ralph," she said, "why don't you sell him one of your extra ones?"

"Look, Aimee, do I tell you how to run your hoop circus?"

"How much do those mirrors cost?"

"I can get 'em secondhand for thirty-five bucks."

"Why don't you tell him where he can buy one, then?"

"Aimee, you're not smart." He laid his hand on her knee. She moved her knee away. "Even if I told him where to go, you think he'd buy one? Not on your life. And why? He's self-conscious. Why, if he even knew I knew he was flirtin' around in front of that mirror in Screwy Louie's Room, he'd never come back. He plays like he's goin' through the Maze to get lost, like everybody else. Pretends like he don't care about that special room. Always waits for business to turn bad, late nights, so he has that room to himself. What he does for entertainment on nights when business is good, God knows. No, sir, he wouldn't dare go buy a mirror anywhere. He ain't got no friends, and even if he did he couldn't ask them to buy him a thing like that. Pride, by God, pride. Only reason he even mentioned it to me is I'm practically the only guy he knows. Besides, *look* at him—he ain't got enough to buy a mirror like those. He might be savin' up, but where in hell in the world today can a dwarf work? Dime a dozen, drug on the market, outside of circuses."

"I feel awful. I feel sad." Aimee sat staring at the empty boardwalk. "Where does he live?"

"Fly trap down on the waterfront. The Ganghes Arms. Why?"

"I'm madly in love with him, if you must know."

Ralph grinned around his cigar. "Aimee," he said. "You and your *very* funny jokes."

A warm night, a hot morning, and a blazing noon. The sea was a sheet of burning tinsel and glass.

Aimee came walking, in the locked-up carnival alleys out over the warm sea, keeping in the shade, half a dozen sun-bleached magazines under her arm. She opened a flaking door and called into hot darkness. "Ralph?" She picked her way back through the black hall behind the mirrors, her heels tacking the wooden floor. "Ralph?"

Someone stirred sluggishly on a canvas cot. "Aimee?"

He sat up and screwed a dim light bulb into the dressing table socket. He squinted at her, half blinded. "Hey, you look like the cat swallowed a canary."

"Ralph, I came about the midget!"

"Dwarf, Aimee honey, dwarf. A midget is in the cells, born that way. A dwarf is in the glands…"

"Ralph! I just found out the most wonderful thing about him!"

"Honest to God," he said to his hands, holding them out as witnesses to his disbelief. "This woman! Who in hell gives two cents for some ugly little—"

"Ralph!" She held out the magazines, her eyes shining. "He's a writer! Think of that!"

"It's a pretty hot day for thinking." He lay back and examined her, smiling faintly.

"I just happened to pass the Ganghes Arms, and saw Mr. Greeley, the manager. He says the typewriter runs all night in Mr. Big's room!"

"Is *that* his name?" Ralph began to roar with laughter.

"Writes just enough pulp detective stories to live. I found one of his stories in the secondhand magazine place, and, Ralph, guess what?"

"I'm tired, Aimee."

"This little guy's got a soul as big as all outdoors; he's got *everything* in his head!"

"Why ain't he writin' for the big magazines, then, I ask you?"

"Because maybe he's afraid—maybe he doesn't know he can do it. That happens. People don't believe in themselves. But if he only tried, I bet he could sell stories anywhere in the world."

"Why ain't he rich, I wonder?"

"Maybe because ideas come slow because he's down in the dumps. Who wouldn't be? So small that way? I bet it's hard to think of anything except being so small and living in a one-room cheap apartment."

"Hell!" snorted Ralph. "You talk like Florence Nightingale's grandma."

She held up the magazine. "I'll read you part of his crime story. It's got all the guns and tough people, but it's told by a dwarf. I bet the editors never guess the author knew what he was writing about. Oh, please don't sit there like that, Ralph! Listen."

And she began to read aloud:

"'I am a dwarf and I am a murderer. The two things cannot be separated. One is the cause of the other.

"'The man I murdered used to stop me on the street when I was twenty-one, pick me up in his arms, kiss my brow, croon wildly to me, sing Rock-a-bye Baby, haul me into meat markets, toss me on the scales and cry, "Watch it. Don't weigh your thumb, there, butcher!"'

"'Do you *see* how our lives moved toward murder? This fool, this persecutor of my flesh and soul!

"'As for my childhood: my parents were small people, not quite dwarfs, not quite. My father's inheritance kept us in a doll's house, an amazing thing like a white-scrolled wedding cake, little rooms, little chairs, miniature paintings, cameos, ambers with insects caught within, everything tiny, tiny, tiny! The world of Giants far away, an ugly rumor beyond the garden wall. Poor mama, papa! They meant only the best for me. They kept me, like a porcelain vase, small and treasured, to themselves, in our ant world, our beehive rooms, our microscopic library, our land of beetle-sized doors and moth windows. Only now do I see the magnificent size of my parents' psychosis! They must have dreamed they would live forever, keeping me like a butterfly under glass. But first father died, and then fire ate up the little house, the wasp's nest, and every postage stamp mirror and salt-cellar closet within. Mama, too, gone! And myself alone, watching the fallen embers, tossed out into a world of Monsters and Titans, caught in a landslide of reality, rushed, rolled and smashed to the bottom of the cliff!

"'It took me a year to adjust. A job with a sideshow was unthinkable. There seemed no place for me in the world. And then, a month ago, the Persecutor came into my life, clapped a bonnet on my unsuspecting head, and cried to friends, "I want you to meet the little woman!"""

Aimee stopped reading. Her hands were unsteady, and the magazine shook as she handed it to Ralph. "You finish it. The rest is a murder story. It's all right. But don't you *see?* That little man. That little man."

Ralph tossed the magazine aside and lit a cigarette lazily. "I like westerns a lot better."

"Ralph, you *got* to read it. He needs someone to tell him how good he is and keep him writing."

Ralph looked at her, his head to one side. "And guess who's going to do it? Well, well, ain't we just the Saviour's right hand?"

"I won't listen!"

"Use your head, dammit! You go busting in on him he'll think you're handing him pity. He'll chase you screamin' outa his room."

She sat down, thinking about it slowly, trying to turn it over and see it from every side. "I don't know. Maybe you're right. Oh, it's not just pity, Ralph, honest. But maybe it'd look like it to him. I've got to be awful careful."

He shook her shoulder back and forth, pinching softly, with his fingers. "Hell, hell, layoff him, is all I ask; you'll get nothing but trouble for your dough. God, Aimee, I never *seen* you so hepped on anything. Look, you and me, let's make it a day, take a lunch, get us some gas, and just drive on down the coast as far as we can drive; swim, have supper, see a good show in some little town—to hell with the carnival, how about it? A damn nice day and no worries. I been savin' a coupla bucks."

"It's because I know he's different," she said, looking off into darkness. "It's because he's something we can never be— you and me and all the rest of us here on the pier. It's so funny, so funny. Life fixed him so he's good for nothing but carny shows, yet there *he* is on the land. And life made us so we wouldn't have to work in the carny shows, but here *we* are, anyway, way out here at sea on the pier. Sometimes it seems a million miles to shore. How come, Ralph, that we got the bodies, but he's got the brains and can think things we'll never even guess?"

"You haven't even been listening to me!" said Ralph.

She sat with him standing over her, his voice far away. Her eyes were half shut and her hands were in her lap, twitching.

"I don't like that shrewd type look you're getting on," he said, finally.

She opened her purse slowly and took out a small roll of bills and started counting. "Thirty-five, forty dollars. There! I'm going to phone Billie Fine and have him send out one of those tall type mirrors to Mr. Bigelow at the Ganghes Arms. Yes, I am!"

"What!"

"Think how wonderful for him, Ralph, having one in his own room *any* time he wants it. Can I use your phone?"

"Go ahead, *be* nutty."

Ralph turned quickly and walked off down the tunnel. A door slammed behind him.

Aimee waited, then after awhile put her hands to the phone and began to dial, with painful slowness. She paused between numbers, holding her breath, shutting her eyes, thinking how it might seem to be small in the world, and then one day someone sends a special mirror by. A mirror for your room where you can hide away with the big reflection of yourself, shining, and write stories and stories, never going out into the world unless you had to. How might it be then, alone, with the wonderful illusion all in one piece in the room. Would it make you happy or sad, would it help your writing or hurt it? She shook her head back and forth, back and forth. At least this way there would be no one to look down at you. Night after night, perhaps rising secretly at three in the cold morning, you could wink and dance around and smile and wave at yourself, so tall, so tall, so very fine and tall in the bright looking-glass.

A telephone voice said, "Billie Fine's."

"Oh, *Billie!*" she cried.

Night came in over the pier. The ocean lay dark and loud under the planks. Ralph sat cold and waxen in his glass coffin, laying out the cards, his eyes fixed, his mouth stiff. At his elbow, a growing pyramid of burnt cigarette butts grew larger. When Aimee walked along under the hot red and blue bulbs, smiling, waving, he did not stop setting the cards down slow and very slow. "Hi, Ralph!" she said.

"How's the love affair?" he asked, drinking from a dirty glass of iced water. "How's Charlie Boyer, or is it Gary Grant?"

"I just went and bought me a new hat," she said, smiling. "Gosh, I feel *good!* You know why? Billie Fine's sending a mirror out tomorrow! Can't you just see the nice little guy's face?"

"I'm not so hot at imagining."

"Oh, Lord, you'd think I was going to *marry* him or something."

"Why not? Carry him around in a suitcase. People say, Where's your husband? all you do is open your bag, yell, *Here* he is! Like a silver cornet. Take him outa his case any old hour, playa tune, stash him away. Keep a little sandbox for him on the back porch."

"I was feeling so good," she said.

"Benevolent is the word." Ralph did not look at her, his mouth tight. "Ben-ev-o-*lent.* I suppose this all comes from me watching him through that knothole, getting my kicks? *That* why you sent the mirror? People like you run around with tambourines, taking the joy out of my life."

"Remind me not to come to your place for drinks any more. I'd rather go with no people at all than *mean* people."

Ralph exhaled a deep breath.

"Aimee, Aimee. Don't you know you can't help that guy? He's bats. And this crazy thing of yours is like saying, Go ahead, *be* batty, I'll help you, pal."

"Once in a lifetime anyway, it's nice to make a mistake if you think it'll do somebody some good," she said.

"God deliver me from do-gooders, Aimee."

"Shut up, shut up!" she cried, and then said nothing more.

He let the silence lie awhile, and then got up, putting his fingerprinted glass aside. "Mind the booth for me?"

"Sure. Why?"

She saw ten thousand cold white images of him stalking down the glassy corridors, between mirrors, his mouth straight and his fingers working themselves.

She sat in the booth for a full minute and then suddenly shivered. A small clock ticked in the booth and she turned the deck of cards over, one by one, waiting. She heard a hammer pounding and knocking and pounding again, far away inside the Maze; a silence, more waiting, and then ten thousand images folding and refolding and dissolving, Ralph striding, looking out at ten thousand images of her in the booth. She heard his quiet laughter as he came down the ramp.

"Well, what's put you in such a good mood?" she asked, suspiciously.

"Aimee," he said, carelessly, "we shouldn't quarrel. You say tomorrow Billie Fine's sending that mirror out to Mr. Big's?"

"You're not going to try anything funny?"

"Me?" He moved her out of the booth and took over the cards, humming, his eyes bright. "Not me, oh no, not me." He did not look at her, but started quickly to slap out the cards. She stood behind him. Her right eye began to twitch a little. She folded and unfolded her arms. A minute ticked by. The only sound was the ocean under the night pier, Ralph breathing in the heat, the soft ruffle of the cards. The sky over the pier was hot and thick with clouds. Out at sea, faint glows of lightning were beginning to show.

"Ralph," she said at last.

"Relax, Aimee," he said.

"About that trip you wanted to take down the coast—"

"Tomorrow," he said. "Maybe next month. Maybe next year. Old Ralph Banghart's a patient guy. I'm not worried, Aimee. Look." He held up a hand. "I'm calm."

She waited for a roll of thunder at sea to fade away.

"I just don't want you mad, is all. I just don't want anything bad to happen, promise me."

The wind, now warm, now cool, blew along the pier. There was a smell of rain on the wind. The clock ticked. Aimee began to perspire heavily, watching the cards move and move. Distantly, you could hear targets being hit and the sound of the pistols at the shooting gallery.

And then, there he was.

Waddling along the lonely concourse, under the insect bulbs, his face twisted and dark, every movement an effort. From a long way down the pier he came, with Aimee watching. She wanted to say to him, This is your last night, the last time you'll have to embarrass yourself by coming here, the last time you'll have to put up with being watched by Ralph, even in secret. She wished she could cry out and laugh and say it right in front of Ralph. But she said nothing.

"Hello, hello!" shouted Ralph.

"It's free, on the house, tonight! Special for old customers!"

The Dwarf looked up, startled, his little black eyes darting and swimming in confusion. His mouth formed the word thanks and he turned, one hand to his neck, pulling his tiny lapels tight up about his convulsing throat, the other hand clenching the silver dime secretly. Looking back, he gave a little nod, and then scores of dozens of compressed and tortured faces, burnt a strange dark color by the lights, wandered in the glass corridors.

"Ralph," Aimee took his elbow. "What's going on?"

He grinned. "I'm being benevolent, Aimee, benevolent."

"Ralph," she said.

"Sh," he said. "*Listen.*"

They waited in the booth in the long warm silence.

Then, a long way off, muffled, there was a scream.

"Ralph!" said Aimee.

"Listen, listen!" he said.

There was another scream, and another and still another, and a threshing and a pounding and a breaking, a rushing around and through the maze. There, there, wildly colliding and ricocheting from mirror to mirror, shrieking hysterically and sobbing, tears on his face, mouth gasped open, came Mr. Bigelow. He fell out into the blazing night air, glanced about wildly, wailed, and ran off down the pier.

"Ralph, what happened?"

Ralph sat laughing and slapping his thighs.

She slapped his face. "What'd you *do?*"

He didn't quite stop laughing. "Come on. I'll show you!"

And then she was in the maze, rushed from white-hot mirror to mirror, seeing her lipstick all red fire a thousand times repeated on down a burning silver cavern where strange hysterical women much like herself followed a quick-moving, smiling man. "Come on!" he cried. And they broke free into a dust-smelling tiny room.

"Ralph!" she said.

They both stood on the threshold of the little room where the Dwarf had come every night for a year. They both stood where the Dwarf had stood each night, before opening his eyes to see the miraculous image in front of him.

Aimee shuffled slowly, one hand out, into the dim room.

The mirror had been changed. This new mirror made even normal people small, small, small; it made even tall people little and dark and twisted smaller as you moved forward.

And Aimee stood before it thinking and thinking that if it made big people small, standing here, God, what would it do to a dwarf, a tiny dwarf, a dark dwarf, a lonely dwarf?

She turned and almost fell. Ralph stood looking at her. "Ralph," she said. "God, why did you do it?"

"Aimee, come back!"

She ran out through the mirrors, crying. Staring with blurred eyes, it was hard to find the way, but she found it. She stood blinking at the empty pier, started to run one way, then another, then still another, then stopped. Ralph came up behind her, talking, but it was like a voice heard behind a wall late at night, remote and foreign.

"Don't talk to me," she said.

"Aimee, it was just a joke—"

Someone came running up the pier. It was Mr. Kelly from the shooting gallery. "Hey, any you see a little guy just now? Little stiff swiped a pistol from my place, loaded, run off before I'd get a hand on him! You help me find him?"

And Kelly was gone, sprinting, turning his head to search between all the canvas sheds, on away under the hot blue and red and yellow strung bulbs.

Aimee rocked back and forth and took a step.

"Aimee, where you going?"

She looked at Ralph as if they had just turned a corner, strangers passing, and bumped into each other. "I guess," she said, "I'm going to help search."

"You won't be able to do nothing."

"I got to try, anyway. Oh God, Ralph, this is *all* my fault! I shouldn't have phoned Billie Fine! I shouldn't've ordered a mirror and got you so mad you did this! It's *me* should've gone to Mr. Big, not a crazy thing like I bought! I'm going to find him if it's the last thing I do in my life."

Swinging about slowly, her cheeks wet, she saw the quivery mirrors that stood in front of the Maze. Ralph's reflection was in one of them. She could not take her eyes away from the image; it held her in a cool and trembling fascination, with her mouth open.

"Aimee, what's wrong? What're you—"

He sensed where she was looking and twisted about to see what was going on. His eyes widened.

He scowled at the mirror.

A horrid, ugly little man, two feet high, with a pale, squashed face under an ancient straw hat, scowled back at him. Ralph stood there glaring at himself.

Aimee walked slowly and then began to walk fast and then began to run. She ran down the empty pier and the wind blew warm and it blew large drops of hot rain on her all the time she was running.

THE END

THE CHEMICAL VAMPIRE

By Lee Francis
(aka Leroy Yerxa)

He tried to create life; but the body that came from his laboratory was dead…until night came!

"I CAN'T understand it, Mr. Grant. None of the workmen touched the coffin—we were only repairing the mausoleum as you instructed. And I know it wasn't open like this earlier this afternoon…"

The foreman stood, uncertainly at the entrance to the mausoleum, his eyes watching the frowning features of Jason Grant.

Grant was a short, plumpish man, with thin grayed hair and hard business eyes. Many had said they were as hard as the bricks that had made the Grant fortune. Now those eyes, which had guided the Grant Brickyards to a lofty position in industry, were clouded. They stared at the foreman with concealed puzzlement.

"Why should anyone want to open the coffin of Marta Boronna?"

The foreman shook his head. "I wouldn't know about that, sir. Maybe you better take a look at it. There's something else that's mighty peculiar…"

Grant inclined his head. "I'll do just that. But what else is so unusual?"

The foreman turned away. "You'll see, sir."

Jason Grant shrugged and edged past the workman into the musty mausoleum. The air was dank, oppressive. It had about it a quality of stillness, of age. Unconsciously Grant found himself trying not to breathe too deeply. He had the queer sensation that he was drawing the vapors of eternity into his lungs.

He walked slowly across the broad granite floor. His eyes swept the sides of the massive tomb, caressed briefly each dusty coffin resting on its own hallowed niche. Each coffin with an inscription. Each inscription a member of his family for the past hundred years. His eyes by-passed the empty niches. There were no inscriptions on those—yet.

Finally he came to a coffin that lay slightly askew on its stone slab. His eyes narrowed as he saw the lid of the coffin raised and projected an inch or two off its previous sealed position. He read the inscription cut into the stone beside the casket: *Marta Boronna, born 1850, died 1880. May she rest easier in her tomb than they who put her here...*

Grant heard the foreman move up beside him. He watched as the man moved over to the coffin and raised the heavy lid.

"Here, sir, look..."

Grant stepped forward hesitantly.

He did not like to look into the privacy of death. But he noted the insistence in the man's voice and peered over the edge of the casket.

His breath drew in sharply and for a moment he felt a strange wave of fear. Then the fear turned to startled amazement.

He was staring at the slender remains of a skeleton. The bones lay grey and somber, with a skull staring sightlessly up at him.

But it was not the skeleton of what had once been a slender young woman that brought a gasp to Jason Grant's lips. Nor was it the vacuous look of a lonely skull that brought a tremor to his face.

For his eyes were riveted on a narrow, wedge-shaped piece of wood, a stake that stuck in a half-upright position between the ribs of the skeleton. A stake that at one time must have pierced through skin and flesh and bone into a beating, pulsing heart.

"Do you see what I mean, sir? That stake... What does it mean?"

Grant motioned quickly for the man to replace the lid of the casket. Then he turned his back, waiting.

THE CHEMICAL VAMPIRE
By LEE FRANCIS

**He tried to create life; but the body that came
from his laboratory was dead ... until night came!**

The foreman came around him, holding the piece of wood in
his hands.

"What shall I do with it, sir?"

Grant's eyes bulged as he saw the piece of wood.

"You fool! What did you remove *that* for?"

The man took a backward step at the anger in Grant's voice.

"Did I do something wrong? It didn't seem right that this
should remain there..."

Grant forced himself to curb his anger. He knew suddenly that this man would not understand. And he also knew that he was not sure he understood himself. As he stared at the stake in the foreman's hand his mind raced back over his family history. *May she rest easier in her tomb than they who put her here...*

Marta Boronna. Distant member of the Grant dynasty. Marta Boronna, who had been accused of witchcraft and vampirism by the narrow 19th century minds of Kenton, Massachusetts. Marta Boronna who had been attacked one solemn night by a masked mob. Attacked and killed. Killed and quietly buried.

It had only been in recent years that he had removed the casket from its dank grave and placed it beside other members of the family in the great mausoleum he had built thirty years before. He had felt pity at that time, for he had known of her tragic death, though the newspapers had not mentioned the incident at length. Nor had the savage killing of Marta Boronna received other notoriety. It had been hushed up, a thing to be spoken of only in whispers. Sure was the fate of the woman accused of being a vampire.

Now as he stared at the stake that had pierced the heart of the woman, he found that he no longer felt pity stir him. It was as if a strange fear took a grip on his soul. A thing he did not understand. A thing he wanted to ignore, forget.

He sighed finally and looked at the foreman.

"No matter. Throw the stake away. And forget about this. One of the men probably got curious and lifted the lid. The stake might be his idea of a practical joke. But certainly in bad taste."

The foreman pursed his lips thoughtfully.

"I can't see why any of the men would do a thing like that... But if you don't want me to press the matter..."

"Drop it," Grant said decisively.

He followed the foreman out of the tomb and after a few instructions to the waiting workmen to complete the repairs on the roof of the mausoleum; he strode quickly away to the gates of the cemetery and his waiting automobile.

As he got behind the wheel of the car he shut the incident from his mind, remembering that he had planned on dropping over to his nephew's laboratory. There were things he had to say to Hal Grant.

He thought of them as he drove.

HAL GRANT turned from his worktables, topped with strange retorts, tubes with bubbling liquids, and weirdly constructed electrical apparatus.

The knock came again at the door of the laboratory.

Hal walked swiftly over to the door and opened it. He stared down from his six-foot height at the impatient face of his uncle, Jason Grant.

"You took your time in answering," Jason Grant said irately.

Hal smiled. "Still the old bull dog." Then, apologetically, "I'm in a crucial stage of my experiments, I—"

"Experiments!" Jason Grant snorted the word out. "I don't mind telling you, Hal, I'm getting a little tired of all the expense your *experiments* are costing me! This last bill—a thousand dollars! For what!"

The younger man stroked his bearded jaw and shrugged.

"I needed the chemicals. They're expensive, I know, but—"

"Expensive! That's putting it mildly! And for what? In your own words, to reproduce the seventy-nine cents worth of chemicals in the human body! Hah! What I mean is—seventy-nine thousand *dollars!*"

A trace of anger touched Hal Grant's eyes.

"I don't think that's quite fair, Uncle Jason. If you couldn't afford it it would be a different matter. And you know how much this experiment means to me."

The anger left Jason Grant's face. In its place was a studied look of exasperation. He waved his hand around the laboratory.

"Afford it? There's a limit even to my generosity! All this tomfoolery to produce a human body from its chemical components! All this wasted money and effort to satisfy a childish theory and imagination fostered by science-fiction magazines! It's about time you grew up and took your place in the business world!"

Hal's cheeks colored. "Maybe I did read science-fiction magazines when I was younger. And maybe they were all imagination. But then, maybe the atom bomb was also imagination. And rocket flight, and radar, and—"

Jason Grant waved his hand. "We've been through all that before. I'll try and put some sense in your head another way. Just how long do you think Betty Starrett is going to tolerate all this? There's a limit to her patience, just as there is to mine. But she'll have to live with you—if she ever does marry you!"

"Betty understands the importance of my work," Hal said quietly.

"Does she? Then maybe I heard her wrong yesterday when she told me I should use my influence and have you stop meddling with all these fool chemicals!"

"I don't believe you," Hal's voice was sharp.

"Then ask her yourself. She knows as well as I do that it's all a waste of time and money. I—"

"I wouldn't be so quick about saying that," Hal interrupted hotly. Then he paused and a note of eagerness entered his voice. "My experiment is in the final stage. This afternoon I produced a perfect female head—in that retort on the bench! The next and final step is only a matter of hours!"

Jason Grant took a deep breath. "Then you won't stop this nonsense. You're bound to continue making a fool of yourself?"

"Nothing could stop me now," Hal Grant said firmly. "And if it will be any relief to you, there won't be any more bills. As I said before, my work is nearly completed."

Jason Grant snorted. "You're damned right there won't be any more expense! But I'm not through with this discussion. We'll continue it later tonight. I'll be waiting in my study."

He turned on his heel then, and strode from the laboratory, slamming the door as he went.

THE afternoon hours dragged interminably onward. Long shadows started to creep from the open windows in the west wall of the laboratory as Hal Grant worked ceaselessly before a long cloth covered table. His fingers delicately added chemical after chemical to a long metal receptacle that lay on the table. With each addition he adjusted dials and switches on electrical apparatus connected to the metal vat.

Faint traces of smoke rose from the bubbling mixture as he watched and worked, and the hum of an electric governor grew louder as more current was generated and utilized.

Finally he straightened and took a small test tube from a rack. He stared hopefully at the bright blue liquid inside it. Then, his lips forming a grim line, he slowly tipped the test tube and emptied the contents in the vat.

There was a sizzling sound as the chemical struck the bubbling mixture in the vat, followed by a thick cloud of acrid smoke.

Hal Grant stepped back in sudden alarm from the violently reacting chemical mixture.

Then slowly the dense smoke began to fade, and he could see the vat again. He stared open-mouthed, his eyes not daring to believe what he saw.

He was looking at a body.

She lay in the now suddenly still vat, the bubbling liquids dissipated, the hum of the generators a barely audible sound. She lay, a perfectly formed body, from the pinkness of her small well-shaped toes, to the long, flaxen-like auburn hair.

Hal Grant stepped slowly forward, his feet numb on the floor of the laboratory, his hands trembling with awed excitement.

"I did it—*I did it,*" his voice whispered hoarsely. And a look of wild triumph entered his eyes as his gaze swept over the still body in the vat.

Slowly his fingers reached down and touched one cheek. Soft flesh depressed under his touch. Flesh that was cold.

Some of the triumph died from his eyes at that. Her flesh was cold, cold as inanimate marble. Flesh that should have been warm. Flesh that should have been filled with the hot breath of life.

He adjusted the generators again. A loud hum grew into a roar of power. The vat shook with the force of the current surging through it. Then Hal Grant shut off the current and stepped to the vat again.

His fingers touched the cheek once more. And the flesh was as cold as before. As lifeless as it had been.

In swift movements he pushed the table to the far side of the laboratory. He pulled a fluoroscope screen down across the vat and turned the switch. Then he peered into the screen.

Surprise shone in his eyes as he stared at perfectly formed bone structure. But that was all. Where there should have been the shadows of internal organs, there was nothing. Nothing but flesh and bone. Flesh and bone...

He stared for another long moment into the screen then he shut it off and stepped back, an ironic laugh shattering the stillness of the room.

"I succeeded! I've made a body—a perfect human body! But a body without a heart, without a single vital organ! A body of flesh and bone—seventy-nine cents worth of chemical, flesh and bone!"

He listened to his voice utter the words of irony. He listened to his own shattered hopes well out of him in a frustrated laughter.

He sat down in a chair and held his head in his hands, a great weariness sweeping over him...

BETTY STARRETT walked up the steps to the door of the laboratory. She paused a moment and surveyed herself. Her blonde hair was primly set, her make-up just right, and her summer dress new and snug fitting. She had spent quite a bit of time preparing for the evening, and she wanted Hal Grant to notice it.

She knocked at the door.

After a long silence she heard footsteps approach, and then the door opened.

She stared into the weary eyes of Hal Grant.

"—Oh, hello, Betty."

"Well, I must say, that's hardly the greeting I expected! Have you forgotten we have a date tonight?"

A bleak smile crossed Hal's face. "No, I haven't forgotten. Come in."

She frowned at his dispirited manner and stepped into the laboratory. He shut the door behind her and motioned to a chair.

She moved over to it and sat down, watching him closely.

He paced up and down the floor, endlessly, and finally she asked:

"Hal, something's wrong. What is it?"

He turned to her, his face a mirror of dejection.

"My experiment, Betty. It—it's finished…"

A wave of relief flooded her features.

"Oh, Hal, I'm so glad to hear you say that! I was afraid to talk to you myself about it—did your uncle tell you?"

He nodded dully. "Yes, he did. But that's not exactly what I mean."

"It isn't? But you just said it was finished. Don't you plan to take your place in your uncle's business?"

He shook his head. "You don't understand. I said my experiment was finished—completed."

"Completed?" A frown wrinkled her eyes. "You mean you failed…I'm so sorry, Hal, honestly…"

He laughed then. A harsh, bitter laughter.

"Failed? Yes, I suppose you could call it that. You know what Uncle Jason was always saying about my producing seventy-nine cents worth of chemicals in the human body? Well, I've done that—and *only* that!"

"I, I don't understand you, Hal," the girl said puzzledly.

"Come over here," he said. "Look for yourself."

He walked to the far side of the room and stood beside the long table. He pushed the fluoroscope screen away and Betty Starrett walked slowly across the room and stared into the vat.

A sharp cry of astonishment broke from the girl's lips. She stepped back from the vat in a startled movement.

"Hal! It's a body! A *body!*"

A faint smile pulled at his mouth.

"There's nothing to be afraid of, Betty," he said. "But you're right, it is a body. And *only* a body!"

The girl looked at him with awed eyes. "You mean—you mean *you* created this…"

He nodded. "Yes, I created it. But I failed. For what you see is only flesh and bone. Flesh and bone incapable of life. There isn't a single internal organ. Nothing to promote or sustain life. I failed…"

THE girl stepped forward and took his arm gently. Her eyes were tender.

"But you didn't fail, Hal! You succeeded! You showed us you were right. Does your uncle know?"

He turned away from the vat and the body lying in it.

"No, not yet. And I must admit the last laugh will be his. I've spent all these months to produce a perfect body, when I thought I could produce life along with it…"

The girl shook her head slowly, and there was a firmness in her voice as she spoke.

"You must forget about that, Hal. Men were not meant to delve into mysteries like that…life is God's business."

He shrugged: "I suppose I'm learning the hard way. I guess you and Uncle Jason were right all along."

Her eyes softened. "Let's forget about it for tonight, Hal. Let's walk out of here and just think about—us… Do you still want to take in a movie in town?"

He looked at her and suddenly smiled. He could see the earnest look in her eyes. The earnestness that was trying to soften the miserable failure he felt in his heart.

"Yes, Betty, I think that would be what I need right now. I'll be ready in a minute."

She watched as he took off the long white coat. She watched as he ran his fingers through his heavy hair, combing it back with his fingers. Then he put on his suit coat and she took his hand. She stared at the coat pockets, strangely bulky, and laughed.

"You still carry most of your laboratory with you! What dire chemicals are in your pockets tonight?"

He flushed and started to reach for his pockets. "I always forget…"

"Never mind," she told him. "You know movies always give me a headache. Maybe I'll need an aspirin—or something."

For the first time a genuine smile lit his features.

"I'm afraid these wouldn't accomplish the same purpose. They're part of my experiment."

She moved toward the door. "Well you wouldn't feel normal if you didn't have *some* bottles in your pockets, so we'll take them along!"

He laughed and followed her from the room, switching off the lights as he went.

A BRIGHT bulging moon shed a silvery light over the Kenton Cemetery. Its somber glow played softly through the trees and across the endless rows of tombstones, beating an iridescent path to the silent mausoleum.

Only the faint whisper of the night wind rustling the leaves of the trees stirred the silence. Then even the wind suddenly died away and there was nothing.

As if the wind's departure had been a signal, a sound suddenly broke the night air.

It was a grating sound. The sound of stone being moved. A heavy wearisome sound. Startling and dread in the silence.

Then there was another sound. A low uttering wail of agony. A sound that crept from the bowels of space. A sound that was not of life.

The wind was still silent. It was as if it had run in fear of what was about to occur. As if it had had a warning.

A cloud drifted across the face of the moon, obscuring its light. And as the heavens themselves seemed to turn away in sudden fear, a strange rustling whisper drifted from the stone mausoleum.

And with the whisper came a strange vaporous shape, floating through the iron grating of the tomb's door. It was wispy, the fragmentary shape of a thing indescribable.

Again the low wail echoed hollowly through the night.

For a long moment the wraith-like shadow floated before the door of the tomb. Then, as if it were being carried by the silent wind, it moved.

Out across the tombstones. Through the shuddering limbs of the frightened trees. Across the wall of the cemetery.

It moved more swiftly now. Over fields, across roads, past houses where light streamed from friendly windows.

And finally it reached its destination. It hovered in the air over a brick building, studying it.

Then it slipped lower and hung searchingly beside an open window in the west wall.

It seemed to be peering into the room. It seemed to be studying the rows of benches with crucibles, retorts, and electrical apparatus.

And then it seemed to see a long table with a metal receptacle.

And again the low wail smote through the night.

Then there was silence and the wraith floated through the window and over to the vat.

A body of flesh and bone lay cool and quiet, staring up at the wraith with sightless eyes.

A sound came again. But no longer a wail. It was now a sound of sighing content.

The wraith lowered itself into the vat.

…And shortly, the body moved.

IT WAS very late when Hal Grant turned his key in the lock of his uncle's home. As he moved into the hall and closed the door behind him he glanced at his wristwatch. It was well after three in the morning.

But strangely he did not feel tired. He felt buoyant, almost exuberant. Already the thought of his laboratory failure to produce life to the chemical body seemed nearly unimportant. Betty had done that.

He smiled to himself as he recalled the pleasant hours he had just spent with her. And the thought was even more pleasant, of the many years ahead that were waiting for them both. For he had asked her to marry him. And her eyes had lit up with a lover's light and she had fallen into his arms, whispering into his ear the things that lover's whisper.

And then he had left her at her home, the house her parents had left her when they died. It would soon be their house. He smiled at the thought. He would have his own home then. And Betty…

"Hal? Is that you?"

Hal's thoughts ended abruptly as he heard his uncle calling from the library. He frowned to himself as he heard Jason Grant's voice. Surely he hadn't sat up all night waiting for him to come home? Was he really going to continue the discussion of the afternoon?

"Hal! Come in here!"

There was an urgent note in Jason Grant's voice. Something that made Hal Grant hurry from the hallway and into the library.

Jason Grant was pacing nervously up and down the long luxurious rug of the library, his hands gripped tightly behind his back, his face a worried study as Hal looked at him.

"Is anything wrong?" Hal asked quickly.

Jason Grant stopped his nervous pacing and faced his nephew. Now Hal could see the older man's eyes. They were wide, almost fearful.

"That is putting it mildly," Jason Grant replied. "The town of Kenton has suddenly gone mad!"

Hal looked at him puzzledly. "What are you talking about?"

The older man's lips narrowed in a grimace. "In the past two hours a wave of killings have broken out! Four men are already dead—and all of them were employees of mine!"

A startled look crossed Hal's face. *"Killings?* Four men?...But who?—and why?..."

"That's just it! The police don't know! All of them were found near their homes—dead or dying—from loss of blood!"

"You mean they were stabbed?"

Jason Grant shook his head. "No, they weren't stabbed—at least not with a knife. Each man had teeth marks on his throat, where something had bitten them and drained the blood from their bodies..."

Hal looked at his uncle closely. "If this is your idea of a joke..."

"Joke!" Jason Grant gasped the word out. "I only wish it were! For what I'm thinking is so utterly fantastic that I'm frightened with the very thought! If I'm right, I'm the only person who knows the truth behind these deaths—and I may be on the list myself!"

Hal Grant stepped forward and steered his uncle to a chair. Then he pulled up another chair and sat down facing him.

"Now maybe you better tell me just what you mean," he said evenly.

THE older man looked at him and sighed. "The men who were killed were members of a crew I had repairing the family mausoleum. You probably remember the family history about Marta Boronna...?"

Hal nodded slowly. "Yes, but—"

"Well, *her* coffin was open this afternoon. And the foreman removed a *stake* that had been driven into her heart—the treatment superstition says will end a vampire's existence…"

Hal's eyes looked shocked. "You're not trying to tell me you believe that a vampire—"

"That's exactly what I'm trying to tell you! Go ahead, call me insane! But then tell me how else these men died! And besides, there's proof…"

"What proof?"

"One of the men, the foreman, gasped out the fact that he had been attacked by a woman. A naked woman! A woman with long auburn hair—a woman whose flesh was cold when she touched him—when her teeth sank into his throat!"

Hal Grant sat unmoving in his chair. His breath had caught in his throat, and something tightened around his heart. *A naked woman—whose flesh was cold…with long auburn hair.*

"My God!—It's impossible!" The words gasped from Hal Grant's lips.

"I know it's impossible! And how can I tell the police?"

Hal looked back at his uncle. The dread feeling was great in him now as he spoke.

"I didn't mean about your vampire theory—I meant that the woman you just described is my own creation!"

"Your what?"

Hal blurted out in short, nervous sentences, the events of the afternoon. He watched his uncle's eyes expand in astonishment as he told of the partial success of his experiment. Finally:

"—but she wasn't alive! She couldn't have been alive! I would have known it!"

Jason Grant was on his feet. "Well there's only way to find out about this! If you're lying to me…"

"Why should I lie? I tell you I created a synthetic woman!"

"Very well, we'll see. We're going to your laboratory right now!"

Hal Grant nodded, and followed his uncle across the library floor.

HAL fitted his key into the lock and opened the door of the laboratory. He stepped inside and switched on the lights.

Behind him, Jason Grant walked into the room, his eyes searching.

"It's over there," Hal said, pointing to the far side of the room where the long table stood with the metal vat on it.

He led the way over to it, and stopped a few feet from it, a hoarse cry leaving his lips.

"It's gone! The body's not here!"

Jason Grant edged around his nephew and stood staring at the empty vat. When he turned to his nephew his eyes were grim.

"You mean there was a body—a woman's body that you created in this vat when you left here this evening?"

Hal nodded, the dread closing around him in a wave now.

"That's exactly what I mean! Betty was here—she saw it! But it was dead—I know it was dead!"

"Dead bodies don't get up and walk away," Jason Grant said.

A horrified look entered Hal's eyes. "Then the only other answer is that she wasn't dead... I must have been wrong—there must have been life in her, life that fanned itself after we had left. Good heavens! Do you realize what I've done?"

Jason Grant looked from the empty vat back to his nephew.

"I realize that we've got to tell the police about this! Before anything else happens—"

His voice broke off as the telephone on Hal Grant's desk began to ring.

The two men looked at each other for a long moment. There was something in both their eyes, a shadow of fear, a dread of the unknown. Finally Hal tore his gaze away and strode over to the phone. He picked up the receiver.

"Hello?"

"...Hal..."

The sound of Betty Starrett's voice came across the wire, and the tension left Hal's body.

He turned to his uncle. "It's Betty."

Then he spoke into the phone. "Yes, Betty? I thought you'd be asleep."

"...Hal..."

His name again. And this time he noticed that there was a strange sound to the girl's voice. A hesitancy about it, a tiredness, a—

"Betty! Is anything wrong?" Anxiety was in his voice.

"...Feel so strange...Hal...She was here...Attacked me...throat...feel strange...dizzy..."

Terror closed over Hal Grant. *"She?* Who, Betty? Who attacked you?"

"...Marta...your Marta...body you made...throat hurts..."

Behind Hal, he could hear Jason Grant swearing as he shouted into the phone.

"Don't do anything, Betty! We're coming right over! We'll—"

His voice broke off as he heard a strange sound over the phone. It was barely audible, a weird sort of wail, but it sent a quiver of dread up Hal Grant's spine.

And then he heard the girl's voice again. Only now she wasn't talking into the phone. Her voice seemed far away, and grew more distant as she spoke.

"...I am coming...Marta...I know...dawn is close..."

"Betty! *Betty!"* Hal shouted the words with a sob in his voice. But the line went dead. A click as the receiver was replaced on the other end.

Hal Grant looked stupidly at the phone in his hand for a single moment. Then he turned to his uncle.

"Betty's been attacked! The creature is over there now!"

Then he was dashing to the door, and Jason Grant ran close at his heels.

HAL shot the car into the driveway of Betty Starrett's home and pulled up sharply behind her parked coupe.

"Her car is here!" he exclaimed to Jason Grant.

The older man nodded as they piled out onto the driveway. "Pray God that we're not too late!"

Then they were running the remaining short distance to the house. They could see that the lights were on in the living room on the ground floor, and as they ran up the steps, they could see that the front door was open.

Hal dashed into the house, shouting.

"Betty! Betty!"

He stopped short in the front hall, Jason Grant panting close at his back. They stood then, listening, the sounds of their labored breathing breaking the silence. But that was all. No other sound. Nothing.

Hal ran into the living room. The lamps were lit, but the room was empty. He ran back into the hall, shouting again.

"Betty!"

His voice echoed into silence. He shot a frightened glance at his uncle. Then he ran up the stairs to the second floor. In moments he had looked into each room, and always the result was the same. Finally he came downstairs again, as Jason Grant walked in from the rear of the first floor.

"She's not down here, Hal!"

"And she's not upstairs—she must have left the house!"

Jason Grant grabbed his arm. "Think man, when she spoke to you on the phone—did she say anything besides being attacked..."

Hal nodded dully. "She mentioned a name. Marta. But my creation didn't have—"

His voice broke off as a stunning realization hit him. He stared wildly at his uncle, and saw the same look of incredulous fear in the older man's eyes.

"Marta?" Jason Grant whispered the name. "Remember what I was telling you—remember Marta Boronna! Good Lord—"

Hal shook his head wildly. "But that's impossible! She said it was the body I created in my laboratory!"

"But she called it Marta!" Jason Grant shot back. "Why, man? Why unless—"

"I remember now!" Hal broke in tensely. "She was talking to someone else just before the line went dead! She said something about dawn approaching and she was coming—she mentioned the name Marta again...!"

Silence fell between the two men then. And their eyes locked in a look of disbelief. A look that gradually changed to one of horror.

It was Jason Grant who finally broke the silence. And when he spoke it was as if he were speaking to himself, his voice coming in a monotone of jerky thoughts.

"The dawn...of course! Marta Boronna was released—she found the body in your laboratory—she must return to her tomb before the sun—"

His voice ended abruptly. His eyes stared fixedly into Hal's.

"And Betty's gone!" the words ripped from Hal Grant's lips.

"We've got to hurry!" Jason Grant exclaimed. "She didn't take her car we may still get there ahead of them!"

And with a sense of dread, Hal knew what his uncle meant. There was a tomb. A mausoleum in the Kenton Cemetery. And in the mausoleum a coffin...

The two men left the house, running for the waiting automobile.

THEIR feet moved in rustling sounds across the damp grass of the cemetery. They moved side by side, their bodies touching, their eyes alert, tense and watchful.

The moon was setting in the distant sky. Its light a faint silvery path of iridescence.

Tombstones rose gaunt and naked in the dissipating night around them. And a soft wind, heralding the approaching dawn, whispered mockingly through the trees.

And then they both saw it ahead of them. Hal Grant fixed his eyes on it, and felt a tightness in his throat.

The mausoleum. Ghostly stone rearing its head through the shadows. A squat structure of death and foreboding.

Beside him, he heard Jason Grant whisper, "Look! The door is closed—we're here in time!"

They advanced upon the shrouded tomb and Jason Grant stepped up to the grilled metal door. He pulled a key from his pocket and inserted it in the lock of the tomb. There was a rasping sound as the door opened then.

They stood on the threshold for a moment, staring into the musty interior of the mausoleum. And as they stared, Hal's eyes fastened on a wedge-shaped piece of wood lying on the floor just inside the door. Jason Grant stepped around him and picked up the stake. Then he walked into the mausoleum and Hal followed him.

They stood finally before the coffin of Marta Boronna. They looked through the murky shadows, breathing in the damp, musty air. Only the sound of their breathing broke the stillness now. And each breath they took had an odd weirdness about it.

Hal stared at the open coffin. Stared at the crookedly placed lid, hanging on an angle over the casket. A chill gripped him then. And he heard his uncle's voice beside him. Heard again the low monotone of sound from Jason Grant's lips.

"You may have a new body, Marta Boronna, but I'll drive this stake into your heart—and this time when you die, I'll do what should have been done decades ago..."

As Jason Grant's words trailed off, Hal stared at him. He looked at the stake in his uncle's trembling fingers. And then suddenly he remembered.

"The body, Uncle Jason—you can't kill it with a stake—"

Jason Grant turned to him in the murky light of the tomb. His voice came grimly. "This may seem like witchcraft, Hal, but I know the truth—even if you refuse to believe it. The only thing that will end the life of this vampire is a stake through the heart..."

"But that's what I mean," Hal's voice whispered insistently. "The body I created has no *heart!* It's only flesh and bone—it's—"

Hal's voice died away as a sound crept through the greying night outside the tomb. He gripped his uncle's arm in warning and they turned to face the door of the mausoleum.

Outside they saw a vague shadow move. Then they both moved silently into a corner of the chamber, their eyes fixed in weird fascination on the open door.

A gust of wind eddied through the opening, swirling dry, scuttling leaves before it. And then the shadow loomed larger. It blocked the open door, a silhouette of greyness. And then it moved into the tomb, and a sharp cry locked itself in Hal Grant's throat.

It was Betty Starrett.

HAL'S eyes stared at her in a grim fascination. The girl was clad in a thin housecoat. Underneath it he could see she was wearing pajamas. Her feet were moving slowly forward into the tomb, scraping across the stone floor, her slippers making a scuffling slide of sound.

Beside him, Hal felt the tight fingers of Jason Grant close around his arm as he started to rise. He tensed then, in his crouched position, watching, his breath a barely audible sound.

"We are here…Marta…you must hurry…the dawn…"

Hal heard the dull words leave the girl's lips. She spoke as if she were in a trance. And her feet moved toward the coffin of Marta Boronna as if guided by some unseen hands.

Then the girl stopped. She stood in the murky light a few feet away from them, her back to them, swaying uncertainly on her feet.

In the sudden complete silence Hal felt the cry locked in his throat starting to slip out. He wanted to rush to his feet, gather the girl in his arms, shake the evil power that was holding her from her body.

But he didn't move. He crouched in the grey light of the tomb, feeling the fingers of his uncle tighten again on his arm.

And then there was another sound. A sound that brought a chill of fear to Hal Grant's soul. It was the same sound he had heard on the telephone when he had talked to Betty. It was a wail, a low, moaning sound that rose on the early morning wind.

He felt Jason Grant tremble beside him in sudden tension. And then, as he looked back to the door of the tomb, Hal saw another shadow moving through the grey light.

Once again there was a rustle of swirling leaves in the tomb entrance. And then the shadow loomed into the opening, and stood there.

Hal's eyes bulged in amazement as he saw the shadowed contours of the body he had created in his laboratory that very day. He saw the long flowing hair falling down over bared shoulders. And the sound came again.

From the lips of the synthetic body it came. A weird wail of eerie tones.

And then the body moved into the tomb, advanced slowly upon the swaying figure of Betty Starrett. Advanced with upraised arms.

"We are in time, Betty Starrett. But we must hurry. Have no fears. You will feel no pain. Your life will ebb and you will be free. Your body will then be mine…"

Beside Hal, Jason Grant rose to his feet with a hoarse cry. He stepped forward, the stake raised over his head.

"Stop! You fiend—I'll send you back to the hell you came from!"

The words were a sharp cry, and then Hal was on his feet, tensing his body for a lunge forward.

The creature turned in shocked surprise. And as the two men took their first steps toward it, a harsh laughter broke through the tomb, echoing hollowly.

One arm pointed toward Jason Grant and the older man stopped in his tracks, the stake still held grotesquely over his head. Hal took one more step forward, and then felt a pair of glowing eyes fasten on his.

He stared into the face of the body he had made, into a pair of eyes that seemed to swell and envelop him. He tried to tear his gaze away, but couldn't. And as he stared, a numbness seemed to creep through him, and his feet refused to move across the floor. His arms dropped to his sides like leaden weights, and he stood swaying on his feet, suddenly incapable of movement.

The laughter came again.

"Fools! So you know my secret! You who made this body I now possess! Well, it will avail you little! You will die like the others...but not before I possess the body of this girl!"

Her eyes burned into Hal's. "It is unfortunate that you could not have created a living body for me. And you," she turned her burning gaze at Jason Grant, "are fool enough to think your stake can end my life? Do you not know the body I possess has no heart?" The laughter came again, a triumphant sound that echoed in Hal Grant's ears. "There is nothing that can destroy me now! The world will learn of me—I have a score to settle with all mortal beings! I was killed as a vampire many years ago—but now I am free! Watch closely before you both die!"

THE creature turned from them then and advanced once more upon the swaying figure of the girl.

Hal Grant's eyes followed the slow deliberate movements as the body moved closer to the girl, as the arms of the creature upraised, and the lips opened and white teeth flashed in the grey light.

He fought then. His mind roared with the force of his will. He must break the trance that held him. *He must break it!*

Time stood still then. And the thought pulsed through him, set his blood throbbing in his temples. And slowly his hand moved. Slowly, and then faster. It closed around a bottle in his coat pocket, and then it withdrew. Sweat stood out in cold beads on his brow as he forced his other hand to move.

Then his fingers closed around a glass stopper in the bottle. There was a grating sound as the stopper came away and fell with a clatter of sound to the stone floor.

The creature turned abruptly as its arms reached out to enfold the girl's swaying body. Its glowing eyes fastened on Hal Grant's fingers, swept up in startled fear to his face.

Hal felt those glowing orbs fasten on his. He knew that in a moment he would be engulfed by the terrible power of those eyes.

With every facet of his mind he willed his hands to move. Upward, out. Upward, out.

Slowly they moved. And as they moved, the creature let a cry of fear slip from its lips. The eyes burned a hypnotic force at Hal Grant.

But they were too late.

Hal's hands shot outward suddenly, and a spray of liquid left the bottle.

It engulfed the synthetic body and there was a sudden hissing sound. A cry of agony left the creature's lips and it staggered backward. Then the hissing grew in volume and wisps of smoke puffed from the flesh under the reacting liquid.

The smoke grew denser, obscuring the body, and tiny licking flame tongues leaped through the grey light of the tomb.

Then the hissing faded away and the smoke vanished.

Hal Grant stared at a small wavering mass of ash in the air before him. Then even that dissipated. Until there was nothing.

Nothing but a distant wail. A tortured sound of a lost soul. An agony of sound that receded into the abyss of eternity.

And silence.

A hoarse sob brought Hal Grant to his senses. He wheeled, seeing the figure of Betty Starrett collapsing to the floor. He reached out with his arms and caught the girl's falling body. Then he held her close to him.

"It's all over, Betty. You're all right now. It's all over…"

Beside him, he saw Jason Grant wiping his brow with his hand. There was a dull look in the man's eyes, a look of disbelief.

The girl stirred in Hal's arms.

"I knew what was going on—oh, Hal, it was terrible! I couldn't control my body…"

"I know," he said gently. "But it's all over. You're safe. She's destroyed forever."

Jason Grant's voice came hoarsely. "But how…"

Hal smiled grimly. "I dissolved her. I carried a chemical reacting agent in my pocket…an old habit of mine…"

The girl stirred in his arms, her eyes tearful. "It was horrible, that creature…"

Hal nodded and tightened his grip around her. "I know, Betty, but I've learned that you can't dabble with science—like I did. Man wasn't meant to learn such things…"

"Then you won't experiment again? You'll join your uncle, and you and I will—"

"If Uncle Jason still wants me, yes. I promise you."

And beside them, Jason Grant sighed, relief and sudden content in his eyes as he smiled down at them.

THE END

DR. ADAMS' GARDEN OF EVIL

By Fritz Leiber

*Full many a flower is born to blush unseen, wrote Alexander Pope.
What witchery gave him the foresight to know about the secret cellar in
which was planted...*

TAGGART ADAMS—Tag to a few other millionaires in the magazine world and to the top echelon of his staff—glared across the jade parquetry of his desk and ten yards of tiger-skin carpeted publisher's office at the jasper-inlaid pneumatically-snubbed door, which Erica Slyker had nevertheless just now managed to slam on her exit.

From twelve frosted rear-illuminated glass panels in the walls, eleven superb Kittens-of-the-Month in penultimate stages of undress ogled down at him eagerly, but they might as well have been in neck-to-toe Mother Hubbards or black shrouds and executioner's masks for all the notice they got from Tag.

A deep flush of rage and shame suffused his normally leering stout-Satan's face as his memory replayed the last side of his conversation with Erica:

ERICA SLYKER: Being Kitten-of-the-Month ruined my sister! I would no more consider—

TAG ADAMS: Ruined? Ridiculous! No one laid a hand on Alice while she was here. I still offer you—

ERICA: *(fiercely):* Perhaps it would have been better if they had! This six-story pad of yours is plastered with sex, but there's not an ounce left of the genuine man-woman article. Power-drive and fear-drive have seen to that.

TAG: I'll overlook those bad-tempered remarks. Miss Slyker, I'm sorry as you are that several weeks *after* she was resident here, your sister suffered some sort of illness that—

ERICA: Alice went into a five-day coma! She awakened from it with an empty child-mind, eaten with vanity, all talents lost, fodder for the mental hospital! Lobotomized mind! Vegetable mind! *(Rises from leopard-upholstered chair and points at a Kitten resembling herself.)* And you still dare flaunt her picture? *(Seizes a massive silver ashtray and hurls it at the offending panel, which shatters, the flesh-pink shards clinking softly down on the wall-to-wall tiger-skin and inside the illumination recess.)* Ha! Witch Queen's curses on you!

TAG *(coolly):* I trust you've entirely discharged your infantile angers and will now hear wisdom. Your criminally destructive action I pardon—I like Kittens to have a *little* tiger in them. I *still* offer you—

ERICA: Pah! Sooner than be photographed for *Kittens* magazine with one shoulder strap slipped, I'd make love to you! Ah! That frightens you, doesn't it? I rather thought it would. Good day, Mr. Adams! (Exits, *slamming jasper door.*)

TAG ADAMS took a very deep breath, slowly let it out, then looked down at the seven large glossy color prints neatly spread on the finely-mortised jade of his desk. Each showed Erica Slyker in a pearl-worked pearl-gray suit that beautifully set off her long lustrous blue-black hair. Each was posed against a background of jungle-leafed indoor greenery. In each the long pale face bore an expression of infuriating haughtiness, the short, bee-stung lips puckered in smiling contempt, the high-arched brows lightly pinching between them a queenly frown.

He selected the photo that seemed haughtiest, then methodically crushed the other six in his gardener's left hand, as a first-beard adolescent crushes beer cans, and tossed the jagged balls into a tiger-skin wastebasket.

Then he hurried to the chair Erica Slyker had occupied, scanned its fabric at close range, and finally with a grunt of satisfaction picked up something from the leopard skin between his middle finger and thumb.

Full many a flower is born to blush unseen,

wrote Alexander Pope.

What witchery gave him the foresight to know

about the secret cellar in which was planted . . .

DR. ADAMS' Garden of EVIL

By FRITZ LEIBER

Illustrator BIRMINGHAM

Returning to his desk, he deposited in a small white envelope a single long lustrous blue-black hair, closed the envelope and clipped it to the uncrumpled color print.

"*She* prate of witchcraft?" he breathed softly. "Ho!"

He rummaged rapidly through a couple of drawers until he found the color print of a rising red-headed young female off-Broadway dramatic talent who had recently refused to become America's Crown Princess of Sex Kittens for thirty days and he checked the envelope clipped to it to make sure three green nail

clippings were still there. Next he thrust both prints in a large
manila envelope, tucked it under his left elbow, and hurried
through the jasper door. Then he was hastening along the

deluxe vari-colored corridors of what one recklessly irreverent columnist called "Kitten Kastle" and, eschewing the gilded openwork antique elevator, down the rainbow flights of stairs with their shadowed kiss-niches and half curtained woo-booths, which were strictly off limits to both visitors and personnel except for publicity photographs.

It was 7 A.M. and tonight's party was approaching its aseptically orgiastic climax. Two widely-placed jazz bands racketed Dixie and twist towards each other. The corridors were filled with hordes of beautiful girls with daring décolletages and other carefully calculated anatomic exposures and with hosts of sharply dressed, worried, watchful men.

Yet despite the rapid writhings of the dancers and the posturings of the comedians and the chattering rushes of the self-appointed party-energizers, no member of one sex ever touched a member of the other except for the minimum permitted contacts of the dance and the fleetingest finger-touches.

Ever present was the fear that someone would do something the papers or the police could seize on, something *gauche,* like becoming naively romantic or drunkenly ribald.

AS the Lord and Master of Kitten Kastle came trotting along, manila envelope under elbow, each man drew aside respectfully, with a fawning manly smile ready to pop if the ruddy, bald, sharp-bearded Satan's face should glance his way, while each girl assumed her meltingest ready-to-please-milord expression and thrust forward invitingly, but not at all pushingly, her lips, throat, bosom, hip, dimpled knee, or whatever other portion of her anatomy she considered her *chef-d'oeuvre.*

But Taggart Adams looked neither to the right nor to the left. Men irritated him, and as for girls his hypnotist had been trying for the past three years to revive his aggressive male interest in them, with little success. He was hardly the bold lusty wastrel indicated by his beard and tiny mustache, which were merely his variant of G.I. standard for publishers and editors of "magazines for men."

At the moment the only girl who interested him in any way was one with blue-black tresses draping a pale mask of contempt, and she would soon be taken care of in a rather special fashion.

As for the stuff crowding the corridors…well, the jeweled sex-puppets—*poupees de l'amour*—were jigging around the well disciplined dark-suited male marionettes, the tombstones were jumping at an hour when squares went to work…it was sufficient.

Downward and ever downward trotted Taggart Adams. Past the turquoise swimming pool with its bevy of bikinied beauties, each with her invisible guardrail. Past the pool's 25-foot-deep "basement," where a lone girl with aqualung and with silver-blue hair streaming like the beautiful long iridescent deadly filaments of a Portuguese man-of-war glided among the living corals behind the 2-inch thick view window—and in front of which a boy and girl in passionate embrace jumped apart tremblingly at Tag's approach, blanching at the merciless frown he shot them. Finally he was alone in the somber oak-paneled pale-tapestry-shrouded corridor below even the watery basement.

A quick glance either way assured him of privacy. He proceeded to tap an oaken rosette in a quick three-one rhythm. A silvery-tawny panel slid silently aside yielding moist warmth and flower odors. A kind of tangible night billowed out, and Tag slipped inside. The panel closed swiftly behind him.

HE was in an extensive room that was in deep darkness except for a dab of bluish light forty feet away dimly illuminating four photos on a wall and silhouetting just in front of it a table set with a few small earthenware pots, a phone, and handsize gardening tools. But although the rest of the room was black-dark at first sight, there pressed from it an intense aura of femininity.

As ones eyes got fully adjusted, there was the barest suggestion of ranks on ranks of thick-stemmed, leaf-hooded flowers—flowers giving ghostly disturbing gleams of russet and gold and auburn and ivory and rosier hues...or perhaps the suggestion was more of rows of slim living, sleeping dolls hung by their hair deep amid greenery...or...at any rate, most tantalizing and strange and disturbing.

With a confidence born of perfect knowledge of the room's contents, Tag walked briskly to the potting table and went to work. He set the phone aside. From a tiny shelf below the photographs and their bluish nightlight he took a brownish bulging envelope labeled in spidery hand and brown-faded ink "Mimics" (after quickly setting back one labeled "Vamps" which he'd first picked up).

From the almost crumbly-old envelope he carefully withdrew a round black gleaming seed a little larger than a plum's, wrapped around it eleven times Erica Slyker's hair, thrust it two inches deep into the moist grainy soil of one of the pots, and patted the surface flat.

"Requiescat," he said solemnly as he dusted the gritty loam off his fingers above the pot, "but not *in pace.*"

He carefully leaned the color print of Erica face-inward against the pot and drew a second seed from the envelope, but then he grew lazily pensive and his stern expression softened as his gaze went to the four large old photos affixed to the wall. The one figure common to them all was that of a tall elderly lady in the chin-high, wrist-and-floor-long dress of the last century, with a piercing-visaged aristocratic face, the thin beaky nose and narrow jutting chin pointing a little toward each other like those of a story-book witch.

A genuine soft affectionate smile came to Tag's lips, instead of the tight Satan's-grimace he invariably showed the world. It was always so nice and relaxing to be, even fancy-wise or photo-wise, with truly elderly women—sprightly, gossipy, thankful old girls, wittily waspish at times, even vastly malicious, but totally devoid of the insolence of the sex-urge. And then Tag had so many reasons, including the supreme one, for feeling friendly and grateful toward his brilliant Great-aunt Veronica, world-famous as a biologist in certain mystical and un-stuffy scientific circles, who ten years ago had bequeathed him much more than her monetary riches.

HE gently rubbed the second seed between his fingertips and touched the still-bulging envelope with a miser's tenderness as he rested his eyes and his feelings on the four photographs.

First, his Great-aunt, not so elderly, standing with Luther Burbank in a cactus garden.

In the second, very elderly indeed, she was accepting in Tiflis the reverent handclasp of Trofim Lysenko, Soviet proponent of the theory that environment shapes genetic heredity, at some time before that rogue-scientist's nominally voluntary resignation as head of the All-Union Academy of Agricultural Science.

In the third she stood alone and grimly smiling in front of the shut doors of what a brass plate identified as the headquarters of the American Botanic Society. That was the one signed "Veronica Adams, D.S." in the same large spidery script as that on the old brown envelopes.

The last showed her in a Parisian dining room together with a group of quaintly bearded men in full evening dress—all the faces almost flat white from an overly powerful magnesium flash. She was receiving from them the Meta-Lamarckian Medal for her paper, "Seventeen Verified Instances of the Shaping of Plant Development by Thoughts, Symbols, Pictures, and Exodermal tokens."

Tag's expression grew more pensive still and he began to tug gently and rhythmically with the hand holding the seed at his wide-based sharp-pointed chin-beard. His eyes closed and his face grew tranquil. He began to snore very softly.

His hands did not fall asleep, however. After a bit, although his face did not change at all, they went busily to work, planting the second seed without more ado in the second pot, over which he was leaning closely, extracting from its envelope and planting a "Vamps" seed in a third pot just beside the second, finally replacing both envelopes on their shelf.

Then his hands grew still and his face woke up with a shake and a start. For a moment he was frightened, then he realized he'd simply been dozing standing up—he'd been driving himself lately and Great-aunt Veronica was such a pleasantly soporific topic for reverie. Strange, though, he thought, the dazed abstraction he'd felt for a moment had been very like the states of mind he used to experience when his hypnotist had implanted some particularly strong suggestion—but he hadn't summoned the man for the last three months.

He'd had a flash of the same sort of feeling sometime earlier today, he recalled. Yes, it had occurred during the first part of his interview with the abominable Erica Slyker.

But *she* was well taken care of now. In fact *all* his work here was done, he decided after the quickest of glances, and it would come to fruition in due course.

Meanwhile he had no business loitering away a moment more at this time of the month, he reminded himself as he spun around and trotted through the dark toward the secret panel.

There was a sharp *bzzz* behind him. It made him jump—for an instant it activated his old fear of bees, a fear most unsuitable in a gardener, but so deep that even his hypnotist had never been able to counteract it.

Then he realized it was only the phone…and he kept on toward the secret panel. In a flash of intuition he'd know it had to be his Executive Managing Editor and that for once the bumbler had a thoroughly adequate reason for calling him at his secretest number.

There was grueling work to be done for the next five days, and not one moment to delay.

Specifically, *Kittens* had to be put to bed—not stupid pushy cuddle-crazy girls, but something really important…the next issue of a stunningly successful national magazine!

DURING that time Taggart Adams hardly thought once of his secret garden or of the incidents leading up to his last visit there.

During these periods when he couldn't spare time himself, the garden was cared for by an elderly Sicilian deaf-mute of sub-moronic intelligence but absolute trustworthiness with growing things—his ancestors had trained vines and coaxed hedges for the ancient Romans.

But now at last the next *Kittens* was abed on its whirring ink-acrid presses, the first run mercilessly checked and rechecked, and Tag had a full recovery-week to do exactly what he wanted—no parties to appear at, no avidly hopeful new girls to check over, no boringly protracted undress photography sessions, no new geniuses to give a grudging hearing, no V.I.P.'s to bully and charm...and only one or two members, if that many, of his house-or-magazine-staff knowing what he really was up to or even where he really was.

He could canoe-copt through Canada's hiddenmost lakes, submarine the West Indies in his technically-illegal private submersible, dig London, take a whirl through the Continental capitols, shoot Africa with the seventh wealthiest man in the world, study the Swiss banking system from the inside, or simply tend his secret garden...quietly vegetate...

Well, in any case he would start off with a look-see at the last, he decided.

This time when the panel closed behind him, it was "day" inside. Great glowing checkerboards of window-simulating, sunshine-shedding panels in ceiling and walls made him squint. He patiently let his eyes accommodate and after a minute he saw his garden in its full glory.

To either side of the aisle between him and the potting table, row on row of potted plants went back in rising banks of the walls of the huge room. Each plant was like a large jack-in-the-pulpit or love-in-a-mist or fever-tree flower, in that each thick-stemmed bloom was canopied and bowered by great dark green leaves of the sort botanists called spathes and bracts.

But these must be jills-in-the-pulpit, for each green alcove enshrined a flowering slim girl about twelve inches high. Many showed only their faces, though with swellings in the stem indicating where bosoms and hips were developing.

The less developed showed just a tassel of blonde, brown, reddish, or other-colored hair above a green head-bulge, or perhaps the green husk opening enough to reveal pale forehead and tiny darting eyes.

In the more developed the sheath of the stem had split down the front and peeled back, like a bolero jacket or green dressing robe, half revealing a delectable torso, baby pink yet an anatomically perfect replica of some celebrated figure.

FOR as one studied these flower-girls, it became apparent that they were not some exotic genus unlinked to individual humanity. One began to recognize faces and forms.

Here were the opulent or sweetly up-tilted breasts of some reigning screen star. *There* was the profile of a celebrated society beauty, or winsome junior member of a royal family. A few of the more memorable Kittens-of-the-Month were represented, but on the whole the social trend was upward. Not every plant was unique, however. There were several groups of identicals, including three full blooms in a front row which resembled Erica Slyker just enough to make one realize they or their plant-ancestor must have been grown with the help of photos and exodermal tokens of her sister Alice.

A very few of the long-stemmed girls bulged with seeds. These had their eyes closed, but most of the rest were peering about, chiefly toward Tag.

And although they were armless they clearly had more than ocular powers of movement, for a small rustling went through the ranked flowers now, as if a tiny breeze were sifting through the subterranean hothouse, troubling the canopy leaves; stems twisted just a little toward Tag; minute lips parted and there was the faintest shrill sibilance in the air, as of voices almost too high to be sensed at all.

Tag took deep languorous breaths of the varied girl-scent, feeling utterly content.

This was the place where the world was perfect for him, he decided for the thousandth time: the place where girls were not big troublesome bounding meaty things with rights and ideas and desires, but fragile blooms with just enough consciousness and limited life to make them interesting; fragile blossoms, blooms to be potted and repotted, tenderly nurtured, watered and fertilized and sprayed, brought to the acme of perfection, and then carefully hand-pollinated and set to seed, or ruthlessly snapped off and extirpated forever as the whim took him.

Pinning up girls in a million-copy magazine was pretty good, admittedly. But potting them in a garden...oh, how much he owed to his Great-aunt Veronica and her patient largely unappreciated research and her mimic-seeds! What stretches of bliss he'd enjoyed during the seven years since he'd chanced on the black spheroids in her effects and stumbled on their purpose!

ALMOST his sole regret was that he couldn't regrow his Great-aunt herself. He'd tried—he had a daguerreotype of her as a 17-year-old and a lock of her girl-hair—but it had turned out that the process wouldn't work for dead women. Else he'd have had not only his perpetually blooming row of "Veronicas," but his Cleopatras, Madam Dubarrys, Nell Gwyns, Lola Montezes, and Jean Harlows—granting he could locate authentic pictures and/or genuine exodermal tokens, even if only a pinch of ashes. But apparently for a girl-plant to develop properly it needed to "draw on" the living original girl in some obscure vampirish way, telepathic or sub-etheric, who could say?—since even his Great-aunt had had no wholly satisfactory theory.

The effect on the, girl whose seed had been planted with proper picture and token varied greatly. Frequently there was none at all, so far as Tag could discover. Sometimes she would be reported as confined to bed or sent to hospital with a mild undiagnosed fever or in a light (or occasionally heavy) coma, especially during the period of blooming. Such symptoms generally terminated, and the girl returned to her normal life, with the withering and/or seeding of her plant. If Tag continued to re-seed her, as in the case of Alice Slyker, there might be rumors of protracted depression together with periods of retreat in some mental hospital.

Once a Swedish beauty queen he'd terminated (with a hedge shears) had died the same night (decapitated in a traffic accident), but Tag was inclined to attribute that to coincidence. What the devil, he wasn't trying to work black magic or hurt anyone, he was only satisfying an aesthetic impulse, using tools supplied by a very high-minded old lady. No, he wasn't trying to hurt a soul.

Of course condign punishment, as now of the abominable Erica Slyker, was something else again! That thought stirred him from his delightful lethargy and he trotted to the potting table, past rows of Alices and Brigittes and Margarets and Sophias and a single Jacqueline.

He started grinning before he got there. His "Erica" had developed with commendable rapidity. Clearly Anselmo had remembered the vitamin and hormone supplements. Already the face was in full bloom and the bosom had begun to bulge nicely. The haughty archings of the minuscule eyebrows as she glared at him and the petulant poutings of the tiny lips were balm to his injured psyche—and as much so was the thought of her twisting and moaning now on some hard couch or hospital bed while doctors bent over her baffledly; he'd asked one of his earlier victims about her coma and she'd told him it had been filled with horrid half-formed dreams of being buried alive and bound to a stake and subjected to nameless indignities.

"And serve you right, Slyker," he said now to the flower, lightly flicking one pale cheek with a fingernail.

THE resemblance was perfect. The eleven-looped hair and the inward-facing color print had done their work well.

But something was wrong: the second pot he'd planted had no photo tilted against it. Automatically he glanced to the floor and here was the manila envelope, where it must have slipped from under his elbow five days back. He stooped and drew from it the print of the off-Broadway red-head talent with the small white envelope still clipped to it containing the three green nail clippings.

What the devil had he buried with the second mimic seed?

His eyes came up over the edge of the potting table and he looked for the first time at the plant rising sturdy-stemmed from the second pot.

It was topped by a walnut-size replica of his own head, leaf-ruffed. The face, in full bloom even to the wide-based pointy beard, was staring at him anxiously and gaping its mouth, as if shouting an inaudibly shrill message.

His first impulse, an instant one, was to rip it out by the roots and stamp on it.

His second impulse, which was so violent it rocked him back on his heels and sent his clutching hands flying up into the air, was to nurse and protect and watch over the thing as if it were a hundred-thousand-gulden Dutch black tulip—at least!

Veils fell from his mind's eyes. He suddenly saw that only a blind idiot would have blithely attributed to coincidence the Swede's grisly traffic death on the same night he'd snipped her stem at the neck. No, he must cherish the Taggart-plant in every way! My God, what if a blight suddenly struck the garden?—some horrid creeping purple mold...

Or what if he went into a coma now? He'd no sooner thought that than he was blinking his eyes, taking deep breaths, slapping his cheeks hard, and rapidly stamping his right foot on the concrete. Clearly he'd almost gone into a coma a minute before, back at the secret panel. Probably only the high pitch of tension involved in putting *Kittens* to bed had saved him from blackout during the past several days.

The atmosphere of this damned place was soporific! Maybe he should flee to the Canadian North Woods with its clean bracing air—yes, but it puts you to sleep, they say...

And if he were away, people could get at the garden—get at the Taggart-plant! Kidnap it, hold it for ransom, torture it, take a great big shears and... He'd never really trusted Anselmo!

GRADUALLY sanity returned, especially when it struck him that his deep breathing, hyperventilating his lungs, was all by itself about to throw him into a faint.

He shifted his mind into gear and set it to work under a careful throttle. Dimly he could recall now tugging his beard in the moon-blue dark while the second mimic seed had still been in his fingers. Evidently he'd loosened a hair or two and then buried them along with the seed. His body bending over the pot and thereafter its close presence in the same building, had been the equivalent of a picture or more. In any case Great-aunt Veronica herself, according to her papers and notes, had never been certain whether the pictures or the exodermal tokens were the most important factors in the cultivation process.

THINKING about the thing this way, scientifically, began to put it into perspective for him and he grew calmer, though it remained most disturbing to realize that he had been absent-minded enough (or conceivably hypnotically influenced?) to pull such a trick.

Still, the thing was done, and nothing now remained but to see the Taggart-plant through its relatively brief flowering-span (that thought elicited from him a residual shiver) and then just let it wither away normally. Reasonable care should easily do the job. After all, who in the world now that Great-aunt Veronica was dead knew more about mimic-plants than he? He would be his own best caretaker. As for coma, many girls never seemed to suffer it, even during the blooming period. Why should a strong man?

And, what the devil, didn't all truly great research doctors and physiologists try their serums on themselves? He was one of their lion breed now!

He looked down at the Taggart-plant, which—all shouting anxiety gone—returned him such a brash Satan's-grin that he felt greatly bucked up, positively exhilarated…to such a degree that for an instant, but an instant only, he imagined himself down there smirking up at his own moon-big face.

What the dickens, if that brave little guy could keep up his spirits, so could he!

Whistling, he fetched a small red can and carefully watered himself—and as an afterthought, Erica. It occurred to him that he might try an experiment in cross-pollenization when the stems were fully opened. Normally he self-pollenized all his flowers to keep strains true—girl-girl crosses tended toward mediocrity beauty-wise, he'd discovered by repeated experiments. And of course he wouldn't want to produce any true seeds of himself—he'd never feel safe if any such were in existence, no matter how tightly locked up. But his pollen on Erica's gynoecium—it was a tantalizingly attractive thought!

IN his bemused high spirits he even watered the nameless little plant growing in the pot between his and Erica's, but nearer his own. There was a sharp *bzz!* He dropped the red watering can. Damn that phone, he thought as he stooped and righted the trickling can. It had no right to sound so much like a bee coming in for the kill. He must have the tone altered at once— would have had it altered before, except he'd been reluctant to admit his fear of bees was so great.

But that was silly. Bees were his great ineradicable dread, and he might as well face up to it, just as he'd faced up now to the existence of the Taggart-plant. Why, if it weren't for his dread of bees, he'd have long ago tried experiments in insect pollenization. It was titillating to think of bees crawling all over his flower-girls, buzzing lazily from one of the next.

But who the devil could be calling him here? Not more than a dozen people knew this number—the last person he'd given it to had been the President.

A charming voice said, "Erica Slyker here. Hello, Taggart-blaggart-waggart-haggart-sleep-sleep-sleep! Now that I've given you the cue we agreed on, you will answer any question I ask. You will do whatever I tell you. Can you hear me clearly?"

"Yes, I can," he replied in a singsong voice.

"Good. You're in the garden?"

"Yes, I am."

"Excellent. Place a chair by the table so you can watch both our plants. Then sit down in it."

He managed to face the chair away from the table, but it turned out this only meant he had to straddle it, resting his forearms and the phone on its back.

"You're sitting in the chair watching our plants? How's the vamp doing?"

Obediently Tag focused on the little plant next to his own, only now learning what it was. He'd planted two of those horrors six years ago and decided never again—the tendrils of the one of them had strangled a promising Gina, while those of the other had whipped out and caught a little finger he'd brought incautiously close, inflicting tiny but nasty wounds with their microscopic suckers.

"It is doing quite well," he reported into the phone. "The forehead is showing and I can count six…no, seventeen pale red tendrils. They are about an inch long and have begun to wave a little."

"Bravo! Keep watching that plant too. Now hang up the phone and await further instructions."

TAGGART ADAMS obeyed and then Eternity set in for him. An eternity the passing of whose centuries were marked by calls from Erica only to repeat the "blag-wag-hag" formula, whose millennia were each signalized by an additional inch growth of the red tendrils of the vamp.

After about thirty-five hundred years the face of the vamp became fully visible. As he'd long since guessed from the color on the tendrils, it was that of the off-Broadway red-head talent—evidently the picture and the three green nail parings had been able to do their work from the floor, as being the nearest picture-and-tokens available and otherwise unoccupied.

She had a great talent for the evil eye, Tag decided after a thousand years of being glared at. And for writhing her lips back from her tiny white fangs. And for waving suggestively close to the Taggart-plant those wire-worm tendrils that arched around her face like the hair of a Medusa.

Meanwhile the Erica and the Taggart were developing their proper bulges and finally splitting their green stem-sheathes down the front: the slowest and least titillating strip-tease in the universe.

The Erica looked back at him with a contempt that only became more smiling as the ages passed.

The Taggart, on the other hand, grimaced and grinned and winked its left eye at him unceasingly. Tag became dully infuriated with the little idiot's irrationally high spirits—and bored, horribly bored. If that was the way he'd looked all his life to other people...

He felt the ache of thirst and the sickness of hunger, but they were dulled by a titanic listlessness.

A million times he told himself that a man couldn't be held hypnotized like this against his will, surely not after a one-session indoctrination into which he'd somehow been tricked by a mere abominable girl. Not one of the most powerful men in the world, not the sex-puppet master, not the publisher of *Kittens*, not Veronica's Grand-nephew, not the Lord of Kitten Kastle, not the girl-gardener...

A million times a little voice from a dark high corner of his mind replied only, "Blag-wag-hag."

Thrice there were "nights" lasting for many centuries.

AFTER twelve thousand years he heard the secret panel open and footsteps drag up the aisle. Someone stooped and retrieved the red watering can. It was Anselmo, he could tell from the corner of his eye—no mistaking that hand like a bleached ham, that face big as that of a white horse, for in addition to being a sub-moronic deaf-mute, the ancient Sicilian had acromegaly.

Tag tried to shout, to whisper, to beckon with a finger, just to lift one—to no avail. Without even a single curious glance toward his employer, so far as Tag could tell, Anselmo went about his chores.

For decades and scores of years his big shoes scraped the concrete and there came the periodic gush of the tap as he patiently watered and fertilized and sprayed. Twice the phone *bzzed* for a repetition of the inevitable formula, but there was no alteration in the sound of Anselmo's movements. Both times Tag tried to drop the phone on the floor—and only set it the more carefully back.

A third time the phone *bzzed*—much sooner than the once-a-century rhythm called for. A brisk grating voice said, "Tag? George. All ready to pop those lions, boy? Rhodesia's waiting for us." To Tag's horror all he could say was, "No, thanks," and all he could do was hang up.

Finally Anselmo arrived at the potting table and began methodically to care for the three plants there, insensible to Tag's mental screams, even when Anselmo's sprinkling reawakened Tag's searing thirst and they became the inward shriek, "For the love of God, pour some of that in my mouth!"

Anselmo finished with the Erica, the vamp (a bit cautious with his huge hands there as they moved around the foot-long tendrils), and finally the Taggart. Only then did his behavior alter. He stood ox-still and stared for an interminable time at the smirking walnut-head of the Taggart. Hope rekindled in Tag.

Then Anselmo turned and stared for almost an equally long period at his life-size employer. Tag's hope flamed. If only there were some readable expression in that white face big as a washbowl...

Then Anselmo looked back at the walnut-head, puzzledly shook his own in three wide horse-like swings, shrugged his sloping shoulders, and dragged off down the aisle. The secret door opened, then closed behind him. A trapdoor opened in the corridor and Anselmo plummeted into the hottest room in hell—in Tag's imagination.

A mere thousand years and ten phone-calls later, Erica added, "I know the garden's under the pool. How do I get in?"

Tag focused his will and thought, "Sooner than tell you, I'd see myself in Hell. I'd become a pauper. You're the evil woman my Great-aunt Veronica always warned me against. You're the Witch Queen. No."

What he said into the phone was, "Turn right at the foot of the main staircase. The seventh vertical molding to your right. The seventh rosette from the floor. Press three-one."

"Thanks. I won't be long. Incidentally, you are in Hell and there is no pauper-alternative. Oh, by the way, it's about time you were getting out of that body—it won't live much longer, even with you in it. Don't look at the me-plant any more, don't look at the vamp, just look at the you-plant and project...project...project..."

TAG complied. After a century the walnut-head began to bob and smirk in exact time with his own blinking. Then suddenly it grew moon-huge. Looking down, Tag saw that he had grown a large green ruff around his neck.

His first reaction to his realization that he was now in the Taggart-plant was to try and project himself back into his rightful body.

One glance at it changed his mind. That gray-faced elephantine hulk, that moon-topped mountain, looked *dead*.

This tentative information didn't depress him perhaps as much as it should have. He felt a vivification, an unreasoning cockiness, a confidence in his own powers, although he could only move his head and wriggle his torso a bit. Perhaps it was because he was no longer thirsty—Anselmo had watered well and cool moisture pervaded his every tissue.

Also, time had speeded up for him again—minutes no longer dragged like years.

Or perhaps his exhilaration was due to his increased sensitivity. Air-eddies intangible before now rippled against his bare flesh like brook water. A drifting bit of lint bumped him like a paper boat. Colors were brighter—he could see with the fresh-washed vision of a child. Odors were a symphony, chiefly of girl-scents, which he realized he had never properly appreciated before; now he could pick out each instrument in the orchestra.

And he could hear with exquisite precision and clarity. Why, he could even hear what the flower-girls were saying!

"We hate you, Tag Adams, we loathe and despise you," they were chanting, occasionally varying it with obscenities in several languages.

His chest swelled. Why, it was a kind of hymn. No wonder the little guy had acted so happy. Where was that little guy now, anyhow? Absorbed in his own larger consciousness? No matter, just listen...now what was that French girl calling him...?

"Enjoy it while you can," the Erica-plant cut in sweetly.

"Shut up!" he snapped, swiveling his head toward her. My, my, she certainly was as handsomely constructed as he'd guessed she'd be when she'd first entered his office—he decided with an appreciative, quite involuntary whistle.

"How gallant," the Erica-plant replied with a shrug. "Give him a hug for me, Red."

THE vamp, far more supple-stemmed than the mimics, thrust forward between them. The Medusa-face mopped and mowed. The eyes glared white-circled. The white fangs clicked and skirred. And then the inch thick living tendrils whipped around him until they were like a red-barred cage, their tips not quite touching him, until one slowly dipped and drew itself stingingly across his chest...

"Cut it short, Red," the Erica-plant commanded.

There was a distant grating noise. The red tendrils whipped away. The grating noise continued.

The secret panel was opening. Then the tramp of giant footsteps—Tag could feel their almost painful vibrations coming up from the concrete through the table and his pot and his earth.

Erica Slyker had entered the room: a girl as tall as a pine tree, bigger than a dinosaur to Tag, a colossal Witch Queen.

She was wearing a platinum mink coat over her pearl-worked, pearl-gray suit. To the left shoulder of her coat was pinned a big spray of white funeral lilies.

Under her left elbow she carried a small cubical white box, big as a piano crate to Tag. It hummed, as though there were several electric motors running inside it.

Halfway down the aisle she stopped to look at the three Alices.

"Save us, save us!" all the flower girls called to her.

She slowly and rather sadly shook her head. Then she jerked the three Alices screaming out of their pots.

"Kill or cure, my dear," she said in a voice that to Tag was like thunder. "Anything's better than the state you're in."

She stooped, swinging the three still-screaming Alices high in the air and smashed them against the concrete with a heavy thud, the vibrations from which made Tag wince, and left them there.

All the flower-girls grew silent. The pot-jarring footsteps resumed. Erica set down the white box on the potting table and the electric motors added their different but painful vibrations to the others. Tag writhed. He was discovering why his flower-girls had never liked hi-fi the nights he'd played it to them hour after hour, full blast. Erica bent toward him. It was like a face leaning down out of Mt. Rushmore.

"It's not so much fun being a sensitive plant, is it, Mr. Adams?" she rumbled slowly.

"May my Great-aunt torture you in Hell!" Tag squeaked.

"You'll find Erica in Veronica," she replied cryptically. Then she slowly unwound a long blue-black hair from around the ear of his corpse. She dangled it in front of him and said, "There are many variants of the hair formula, Mr. Adams—and more than one way of applying an exodermal token."

Then she dug her fingers into the pot of her own plant, carefully loosened its roots, gently shook them out and wrapped them in a wet handkerchief, then tucked and fastened the she-- flower in the center of her spray of lilies.

Then she looked at Tag across the white box.

"The Witch Gods do not love you, Mr. Adams," she whispered in a voice like distant thunder.

She took the cover off the box. A black bee, yellow-striped and big as a half-grown kitten, crawled out and up on to the rim.

"You signed your will and your death-warrant, you know, Mr. Adams," she continued, "within an hour of our meeting in your office. Signed them in more senses than one."

WITH the *bzzz* of a power lawnmower the bee took off and came circling widely around Tag.

"After all, you've had a long life," Erica went on. "About fourteen thousand years, wouldn't you say?—even if most of them were spent here during the last few days."

Tiny tears of horror trickled down Tag's face as he craned and craned his neck. He'd oftened wondered exactly what the drops of dew on the flower-girls' cheeks had meant.

"I'll be leaving soon, Mr. Adams," Erica said. "You'll have the place to yourself. The lock will be jammed. Anselmo will assume you've set it against him. I'm going to leave the sunlight turned on full—it's the kindest thing I can do for the others."

The bee lit on Tag's shoulder like a six-legged live helicopter. It stank acidly. Of the million screams inside him he dared not utter one.

"Don't be frightened," Erica rumbled. "Bees don't sting flowers—if they're quiet. And the scent of a male plant happens to be irresistible to these bees."

Two more bees climbed to the rim and took off and came circling.

"It's really an honor to you, Mr. Adams," she continued. "Judging from your magazine, it's what you've always wanted to have happen. It should be an exquisite fate, from your point of view."

More bees took off. A second landed on Tag's neck. The first walked slowly down his chest, its sticky hair-fringed feet pricking and tickling almost unbearably, its sting wagging in his face.

"Yes," she explained, standing up, "the bees are merely going to carry your pollen to all these beautiful girls." She spread her arms wide, then leaned forward and finished, "But before they can carry your pollen, Mr. Adams, they have to collect it."

THE END

MOP-HEAD

By Leah Bodine Drake

…along the countryside, from yard to yard, from farm to farm dogs set up a barking.

IN ABANDONED cisterns and old wells, in moldy heaps of straw forgotten in the corners of deserted barns, in reedy pools deep in the woods, in fungied hollows of dead trees, in all such secret places apart from man, strange life engenders, drifts in and takes root and form.

In a place called Yancey's Meadow such a thing grew and waxed and made itself a shape, listened and dozed and waited.

"Dorothy, where are you and Harry Todd going?"

"Just over the Yancey's Meadow to play, Mrs. Trevyllian."

"Not Mrs. Trevyllian, honey—*mother.*"

"Yes…mother."

"Well, don't you all stay long. Daddy'll be home from Court early today."

"Yes'm…*mother.*"

Oh, dear, thought Aline Loveless, will I ever make a dent in that child's affections? Won't she ever forget that I was Mrs. Trevyllian and not her natural-born mother? Little Harry Todd accepts me—at least, he tolerates me. But Dorothy, no.

The stout, pretty red-haired woman watched the two little figures, seven-year-old girl and five-year-old brother, as they moved off towards the fields that lay close by, for the home of Jeff Loveless stood on the edge of the small county seat of Elk-ford.

I declare, she thought bitterly, if I'd known what a chore it would turn out to be, trying to mother a dead woman's children, I might have thought twice about leaving Bardstown to marry Jeff! That's a fine way for a little girl to address her mother—

"Mrs. Trevyllian"—all right, *"stepmother"!* But even Harry Todd says, "Aline." Why doesn't Dorothy go one step more and call me the Widow Trevyllian?

Six months ago Aline had married the lonely young lawyer with the two motherless children, and for six months she had tried, with all her store of natural warmth and kindness, to take the dead Reba's place. She knew she had succeeded with Jeff, and to a degree with his little son. But with the girl she had failed. The child seemed almost to hate her. Nobody had ever hated Aline in her life and the tears welled as she gave rein to her thoughts. The stitches in the apron she was hemming grew dim and she threw down her work with disgust.

"I'm such a softie!" she said aloud, and bent down to lift Mudge to her lap.

Mudge, a chunky Maltese, was the last living link with her former life, and the feel of the heavy little body gave her comfort. "Mudge loves me, at any rate—don't you, fellow?" she muttered to the purring cat as she rocked in the well-worn chair in the dining room's bay window. "I reckon I shouldn't even sit here, in Reba's chair, if Dorothy had her way."

THE noise of hoofs and a rattling wagon coming to a halt at the back gate made Aline wipe her eyes hastily, and by the time a discreet knock sounded on the boards of the kitchen steps, country fashion, she was once more to all appearances her happy, pleasant self. The knock was followed by a rich baritone calling softly, "Miz Loveless? Ah's heah with de fryahs."

"Oh, it's you, Ben! Come in," and Aline moved to open the kitchen door. Ben Pondy, the colored man who owned a small farm on the outskirts of town had brought in his weekly order of frying chickens.

"What nice, fat hens you raise, Ben," she said, as she took the two limp bodies and rummaged in the broken teapot for change.

"Yes'm, thank you, ma'm."

The old man took the money but lingered.

"What is it, Ben?"

"Well'm, Miz Loveless, Ah don't want you to figger Ah'm buttin' in wheah ain't got no call to—but them two li'l chilluns

MOP-HEAD

by Leah Bodine Drake

of Mistah Jeff's—they shouldn't be out yondah in that theah field so much. No'm."

"You mean somebody keeps a bull over there? My goodness, Ben, I'm glad you told me!"

"Well, no'm…not 'xactly bull. But they's that ol' well in de field yondah. Ol' dried-up well wheah they ain't been no house for de Lawd know *how* long."

"Of course they shouldn't play near a well!" cried Aline. "Why, they might fall in! I'll see that they stay away from there from now on."

"Yes'm…'Course, they *might* fall in, though it done got coupla planks laid 'cross it. But Miz Loveless ma'm, it's kind of a funny place, that Yancey's field. Ah come by theah once, right smack in de middle of de evening, sun shinin' with all his might, ever'thing nice and peaceful, and Ah heah a noise like somebody chucklin' and awhistlin' to hisself over by that ol' well. Man, Ah never *did* stop to heah no more! An' Ah ain't never go through that field again—no *ma'm!*"

"How queer! Do you reckon there might be snakes there?" Aline was half alarmed, half amused at the old man's tale. "I'm grateful to you for telling me, Ben."

"Yes'm. Sho' wouldn't want nothin' to happen to Mistah Jeff's and Miss Reba's chillun. Sho' wouldn't go theah my own self."

Illustrated by Joseph Eberle

AS SHE heard the clatter and clop of Pondy's decrepit outfit move away Aline took a yard-rake and went across the narrow lane into Yancey's Meadow. The sun was hot and the strong musty smell of drying grasses filled the August air. Funny, she thought, ever since I've lived in Elkford I can't remember ever seeing any people in this field, not even any cows. Nobody ever seems to come here except Jeff's young ones.

She trudged across the meadow, her short sturdy young body plowing through the long Johnson-grass. Jimsonweeds caught at her skirt and stick-tights to her stockings. Grasshoppers leaped up in alarm as she brushed by their green hidey-holes. A faint breeze wandering aimlessly towards her brought the sound of children's voices talking excitedly and, she thought, a little stealthily. There seemed to be a third voice, with something thick and unnatural about it. It was vaguely unpleasant, she thought.

She could see no one. The insects whirred, joe pye-weed nodded its purpling plumes, the sun beat down. A quick little chill ran over Aline. "Dorothy! Harry Todd!" she called, her voice skittering away across the field like a scared rabbit.

Some way off, where there had been no one, the heads of the two children suddenly popped up from the grass. As they got to their feet the little girl had a sullen look on her pretty face, and the boy looked frightened. They came slowly towards Aline, and she said sharply, "What were you two doing near that old well?" For now as she moved forward she could see the dark opening in the long weeds, the ancient gray boards that covered it haphazardly pushed aside.

THERE was a moment of silence, then Dorothy said, looking anywhere but at her stepmother, "We were just foolin' round. Just sorta walkin' by."

"Walking by? But I couldn't see you—you must have been leaning right over it! Don't you know that you might have fallen in? Dorothy, you ought to look after your little brother better than this!"

As neither answered her, Aline's impatience, always near the surface, got the best of her. "What on earth do you two find so fascinating, anyway, about this place? You and Harry Todd have been kitin' off here all summer! And Ben Pondy thinks there's snakes around."

"Ben Pondy!" Dorothy looked at her stepmother, suddenly scornful. "That ol' cowardly custand! That ol' scairdy-cat! Ain't any snakes in that well."

"Well, you might fall in... And who were you talking to? I'm sure I heard three voices."

Dorothy hesitated, then she replied, "Nobody. Nobody at all."

"Wasn't nobody, Aline," Harry Todd's treble piped up brightly. "Just ol' Mop-Head. He talks to us all the time and— *ouch!*"

"Why, Dorothy Loveless, you kicked your brother!" Aline, shocked, stooped to comfort the boy whose small shin had been given a surreptitious warning by his sister. "And you *were* talking to someone," she went on. "I heard you, and Harry Todd just said so. Who's Old Mop-Head, and why do you tell me stories?"

"He's just somebody we made up, Mrs. Trevyllian. He's just a play-somebody, honest—mother.

Her manner changed. She was all smiles and sweetness as she took her stepmother's hand.

"Harry Todd and I just stopped to peek down that ol' well for a teeny weeny little ol' second—didn't we, Harry Todd?"

"Uh-huh, I reckon so," mumbled the boy as he took Aline's other hand. As the trio moved off towards home the little girl looked up sideways at Aline in an appealing way she had, and said, "Now that Queen Esther's got the misery again and can't come around tonight, can I wipe the dishes for you, mother?"

To have you call me mother, Aline thought, I'd let you break everyone of them, including my big Spode platter. Aloud she said, "Certainly, honey, that'll be a help."

AS THE little party entered the back yard Jeff's car turned into the drive. Not even the fact that the two children tore their hands from hers to fling themselves on their father, leaving her for a moment outside the family group, could spoil her happy mood that the feel of those small hands had induced. Even Ben Pondy's wailings dimmed in the sudden rush of well being.

This pleasant state lasted through a hilarious if rather scrappy supper, result of the absence of the imperious Queen Esther whose reign in the Loveless kitchen was frequently interrupted by her "misery in de back." Not until brother and sister were in bed (after a washing-up marked by only one broken cup) and Aline was sitting with Jeff on the screened-in side porch, did she remember Ben's story about Yancey's Meadow.

"Jeff, do you know anything about an old well over there in that field—the one they call Yancey's Meadow?"

"What, honey?" He lifted his head from the radio's glowing dials. "Oh, that place. Yes, there's a well there. Been there since the Year One. Why?"

"The children have taken to playing there all the time, and I'm afraid they may fall in, or get bitten by a snake, or something. Ben Pondy hinted they might, when he brought the fryers today. He said he wouldn't go through that field himself for love or money. What's wrong with it, Jeff? Outside of snakes, I mean?"

Jeff studied his pipe a moment. "I don't rightly know, Aline," he said slowly. "I never much liked to go through that field as a kid, but I couldn't have told you why. That well's been boarded over, though, as long as I remember."

He stopped to light up. "Tom Bell tried to pasture some horses there once, but they got skittish about something, and one jumped the fence and took off for the woods, and it was two days before they found her. Funny…"

"Well, I want you to forbid them playing there, dear. And Jeff, do you know anybody named Mop-Head? The children seem to know somebody by that name. I never heard of 'em."

"Mop-Head?" laughed Jeff. "I should hope not! What a handle! There's some Moreheads, live up by Tyewhoppety, but that's a sight too far for their kids to come down here visiting of an evening. But about that well—I'll tell the little huzzybugs to stay away from it."

THE radio crackled and sang, the smoke from the pipe mingled with the cloying scent of clematis in the warm Kentucky night. Where the street straggled off into the fields a lonely arc-light swung, its pale glow like a guardian posted against all things that crept or padded or cried in the rustling woods and ferny hollows, and were not of man. And off in its own place, amid the scummy water and crumbling stones, the dead leaves and moldering bones of field-mice, the thing called Mop-Head was awake, ears up in the quiet.

And the children, awake in their beds, watched a yellow half-moon sail up from the dark woods and send a long ray across the floor. The house was still. The big folks had gone to bed. A whispering began: "Harry Todd, you awake?" "Uh-huh." "Well, get up! We gotta go to the field. We promised ol' Mop-Head."

"I'm scared. He's ugly. He's uglier'n a scarecrow."

"I know—but he's our friend, and he'll do what we want about—*you* know—if we get him things. He promised us, that time we woke him up. He can't do everything by himself—he *told* us that! Hurry up!"

Quietly, as if with much practice, the two children got out of bed and stole downstairs to the dark kitchen. The girl took a large covered plate from the refrigerator, and as carefully as two little animals on the prowl, brother and sister left the house and headed for Yancey's Meadow. Through the milky river-mist that lay in long veils over the grass, they went straight to the well in the far corner. Pulling and tugging, they removed the rotting planks to one side, and tipped over the plate's contents into the darkly gleaming depths.

A wind ruffled the fair hair of the two young heads. A hunting owl called from the hedge, and a fox, passing on some private business of his own, stopped and lifted a startled paw. And that which lived and had its curious being in the well chuckled with pleasure and all its small mouths slobbered as it noisily feasted.

WHEN Aline discovered her loss next morning she was only annoyed and puzzled at first.

"Who took those chickens out of the ice-box?" she asked at breakfast.

"Not guilty. Don't look at me!" said Jeff, busy with ham and eggs.

"Well, somebody did. Those hens couldn't walk off by themselves. And Queen Esther hasn't been here for almost a week—and I doubt if even she would make off with two whole dressed chickens, although I'm well aware of her small-scale pilfering from the larder." Aline turned to the children. "Do you youngsters know anything about it?"

Downcast eyes and absorption in their breakfast of brother and sister told the young woman that she was getting warm. "Come to think of it," she went on, "seems like a lot of food has been disappearing around here lately. Half a coconut cake that vanished over night—just like those fryers—and other things. Come on, kids, 'fess up. Which one did it, and what for?"

"Didn't take 'em," muttered the girl, while the little boy buried his nose still deeper in his milk mug.

"I'm sorry to say this—but, Dorothy, I don't believe you," said Aline, hoping desperately that she didn't sound like the mean stepmother of fiction. Her fear was realized as her husband said quickly, "Oh, come now, Aline! If Dolly says she didn't take them, I'm sure she didn't. Dolly, baby, speak up and tell the truth, the whole truth and nothing but the truth, so help you Moses."

Harry Todd laughed, but this sister burst into tears. Jumping from the chair she ran to her father and clung to him, sobbing, "I didn't, I didn't, I didn't! Oh, Daddy, I want Mommy! I want my *real* Mommy!"

Jeff Loveless turned worried eyes to his wife. "Don't you reckon some tramp may have stolen those hens? What would Doll here want with them, anyway? Tell you what," he added, "I'll go by Pondy's and have him bring you two more. O.K.?"

"Oh, all right," Aline agreed weakly, angry at herself for letting the matter drop so casually. Her thoughts were far from happy as she saw Jeff off to his law-office and heard his last orders to the children to "stay out of Yancey's Meadow." Dispiritedly she turned to the usual chores of the day.

OUTSIDE, under the big sycamore Dorothy pushed her brother back and forth in the swing and whispered fiercely, "Old Mop-Head doesn't want any more dead stuff. He wants somethin' alive next time, he said. Then pretty soon he'll get strong and powerful and can give us our wish...*you* know what."

"Ain't got any live stuff," said the boy.

"Well, then we'll have to find some. That's what *he* wants...and you want Mommy back, don't you?"

"Mommy's dead. They put her in a box," he answered, swinging himself vigorously.

"Silly! I know *that*, Harry Todd Loveless! But Mop-Head can get her back, like we asked him, and then that Mrs. Trevyllian, that ol' red-headed woman, will have to go home."

Her young mind scurried about the house and yard like an invisible mouse, considering all the prospects of living food for their peculiar friend... He had said if he had live food he could bring Mommy back... She tiptoed to the side porch. Mudge was busily washing himself on the step.

When the potato sack swooped down over him the big Maltese was so taken by surprise that neither clawing nor writhing helped him. With the spitting, moving sack bumping along between them, his captors hurried over to the forbidden field.

They pulled aside the boards and looked down. Something glistened a little far below. Dorothy set the sack on the well's lip and pushed it over.

"Yoo-hoo!" she called softly. Mudge made a fine splash.

THE sun shone and westerned. Insects hummed and churred in the warm grass. The shadows lengthened and dusk fell on trees and vines and hedges. Bats stole out of their secret places and field mice ran through their tiny alleys in the weeds. And that which was at the bottom of the well in the meadow felt strong currents pass through its crazy veins, felt the living blood it had tasted nourish the rackety body.

The thing called Mop-Head was not animal or plant or rock, although, by now, it was a little of each. It had no definite body, and it longed for one. A scrap of elemental force that had drifted down over the field from far-off places, and settled long ago in the forgotten well, it had gradually built itself a body and a consciousness over the years. From darkness and silence and damp, out of earth-mold and wet leaves and blown dandelions, of scum and spiders' legs and ants' mandibles and the brittle bones of moles it formed a shape and a sentience. From the thin laughter of children and the far calls of men, from the haunting songs that the winds blew towards its from the Negro church in the woods, from fox's bark and owl's cry and rain's patter, the creature had made itself a clumsy mockery of speech.

It was not good, not evil, and it had one desire: to acquire a solid body. Being an elemental, it had vigor far beyond its size. Now that it had eaten, it felt strong, capable of anything. It clambered up the sides of the well and slipped over. The rising moon glistened on its fuzzy grayness, glittered in its many eyes. Its antenna waved in the warm air and the thing whimpered a little. And in Ben Pondy's hen house, the hens awoke and protested against the strangeness in the air, and along the countryside, from yard to yard and from farm to farm, the dogs set up a barking.

The thing gathered its gimcrack body together and its feelers tested the wind. Finding the direction it wanted, it stood rigid a moment. Then it wobbled off toward the town. And the dogs barked at its passing, telling their masters of what was abroad in the night, and their masters slept.

AS THE Loveless family sat at lunch the next day Jeff talking gaily of a case he had handled that morning, Ben Pondy's old horse came down the alley at a clattering pace and stopped at the gate.

"Mistah Jeff! Mistah Jeff!" The colored man came in the yard at a run. "Come heah quick!"

When the young lawyer let him in the old man grabbed his arm and clung to it, moaning, "Oh, Mistah Jeff, suh! Somebody been at Mizz Reba's grave and mess it all up!"

"In Heaven's name, Ben, what are you talking about? Talk sense!"

"Yessuh, am talkin' sense. Somebody got into you all's lot in the graveyard and dig up Miss Reba. I come by theah jest now, and de grave all open, an'—" He groaned again and clung tighter to the other's arm. "Oh, Mistah Jeff, somebody break open that theah coffin and done stole Miss Reba!"

Drawn by the uproar, Aline and the children stood in an amazed group on the steps. Harry Todd started to cry, but Dorothy, her hands pressed tightly together, grew stiff with some inward emotion. Jeff, without a word and not even stopping to get his car, ran to Ben's wagon. With its owner scrambling up beside him, he sent the ancient horse to a feeble gallop in the direction of the cemetery.

Left alone, Aline felt she couldn't sit home and puzzle herself over the outrageous news. A heavy feeling of unease invaded her. Old Miss Crittenden was a near neighbor, and the young woman decided she wanted the companionship of someone besides the strangely excited children.

"Wash your hands, babies, we'll go over to Miss Sarah's a while."

"Isn't Mommy in that ol' box any more?" asked Harry Todd brightly.

"Hush, sugar—don't talk about it. Your Mommy's in Heaven," said Aline. But she thought she heard Dorothy say to her brother in a low tone, "Mommy'll be back," although such a remark certainly made no sense!

As they passed the side steps she wondered where Mudge was. Her pet hadn't shown up for his usual breakfast of fish-heads. Probably out on the tiles last night and hasn't gotten home yet, she decided with a slight smile.

IT WAS a far from smiling group of men who assembled later at the Loveless family plot in the cemetery. Before the incredulous eyes of Jeff, Sheriff Helm and the posse, which the latter had hastily gotten together, the grave of the first Mrs. Loveless, lay open. The earth was thrown up as if a huge mole had burrowed under it, and the wooden casket, its lid ripped open, and with long scratches on its polished surface, was exposed. Except for the stained silk of the lining, still pitifully impressed with the dead woman's shape, the casket was empty.

Who had taken Reba Loveless from her grave, and why? As the news went around, and the baffled posse explored cellars and alleys and the nearby woods, the question was on every tongue in Elkford. Nobody reported having seen any strangers in town, and there hadn't been a tramp lying-up in a culvert for weeks. And nobody in these parts had any rhyme or reason to do such a thing! By twilight, Sheriff Helm owned himself stumped, and declared it a day until other plans could be made.

"I'll run you home, Jeff," said Deputy Joe Barndollar as the weary men straggled back, in threes and fours, to the courthouse. "We'll start out again tonight, if you say so, but you ought to get something to eat first."

"Eat...! Hell, Joe, I can't eat anything! But thanks for the lift—guess I *will* go home for a while," Jeff said in a tight voice, groaning inwardly. My God, who can have done this to poor

Reba? He longed suddenly for Aline's calm good sense and practical, affectionate concern.

Aline herself was feeling anything but calm or sensible. Miss Sarah had a taste in conversation for rather grisly gossip and speculations. Then, as the word spread from the old lady to her many acquaintances via the phone, with the circle widening as they passed the news along, the jangling of that instrument got to be more than Aline could bear. Several calls to the Sheriff's office had brought no fresh word, and as the afternoon wore on she felt that she'd be better off at home. If Jeff came back he'd be tired and unhappy. Yes, she'd much better go home.

"But I'll leave the children here, if you don't mind," she told Miss Sarah as she prepared to leave. "I don't want them to hear about that grave and Jeff's bound to talk about it."

Old Miss Crittenden was delighted to have company for supper and pressed Aline to stay, too. "You don't want to be in that house alone with Jeff gone, and all the men folks off in the woods and all," protested the old lady. "Anybody who'd make off with a dead woman must be a nasty kind of crook, and there's no telling what he'd do to a *live* one."

BUT Aline had made up her mind to be home when Jeff returned. As she went into the empty street she was surprised to see how far the sun had westered. It's later than I knew, she mused, glancing towards Yancey's Meadow, which was a glory of golden light. For a minute she thought she saw a figure coming across the field towards her, dark against the sunset. It moved quickly, and there was something odd about it. But the light was in her eyes and she could not see it distinctly. By the time she had walked the short way up the street to her house and turned into the driveway she'd forgotten it.

The clematis vines made an early dusk on the screened-in porch and the air was growing cool. She shivered a little, and as she entered the house she heard the back gate dick. She thought the, children must have come home after all. Then a foul smell, unbearably rank and loathsome, assailed her. Rapid, shuffling footsteps sounded on the kitchen floor and a shadow darkened the doorway. Aline looked up…and screamed, and screamed again at what she saw before her.

In its most recent dress, Mop-Head was there.

It leaped towards her, thin arms wound themselves around her neck and pressed. Her senses reeled as she fought the thing with every ounce of strength in her short, solid young body, while the filthy; odor sickened her and the wild horror of it dazed her mind. The pressure on her throat grew harder, waves of pain rolled over her, until one wave, more powerful than the rest, swallowed her up in merciful unconsciousness, and she fell heavily to the floor.

Through the still evening air, down the shady street went a peculiar whistling call. The horses in Tom Bell's stable heard it and whinnied. The town dogs heard it and challenged it fiercely. The Loveless children, playing on the Crittenden veranda, heard it and knew what it was. They looked at each other, and Dorothy said excitedly, "Mop-Head's awake! Come on, Harry Todd, let's go find Mommy!"

The sun was sinking behind the sycamores as the boy and girl ran down the street towards home. A car passed them, and the little boy cried, "There's Daddy!"

Joe Barndollar slowed down and the children piled in, Dorothy crying happily, "Daddy, we're going to see Mommy pretty soon! Our real Mommy, I mean!"

"What?… Good Lord, no, baby!" said her father, horrified.

"Yes, we will—somebody we know is going to bring her back to us—from Heaven, I reckon. He *promised* us!"

"I don't know what you're talking about, Doll," said poor Jeff wearily. "Come in, Joe, I'll ask Aline to fix you a bite to eat. I just want some coffee, my own self."

AS THE car slowed down in the driveway a repulsive odor met them. Could Aline have left a gas jet on? Jeff wondered, although it smelled a lot worse than gas. There was no light in the house, but they could see somebody sitting in the rocking chair by the bay window.

"Look! Look! There's Mommy!" cried Harry Todd, pointing.

Dorothy leaped from the car and tore into the house. The men heard her give a curious gasp and then a strangled cry. They raced in after her, to stumble over the unconscious body of Jeff's wife on the floor. But it wasn't this that made them fall back, holding their arms over their eyes to shut out the horror that met them.

From the rocking chair in the bay window a figure rose to confront them in the twilight. With rotten silk crumbling away from the yellow flesh, with soil and twigs fouling the long, fair hair, with dead eyes upon them in an unseeing stare and dead lips smiling in terrible mockery of life, the body of Reba Loveless tottered towards them. The shredding arms stretched towards Dorothy and the gray mouth opened.

"Here I am!" said Reba.

With a sob of terror Jeff sprang forward to sweep the little girl out of the creature's reach. As he caught her to him, Joe Barndollar took one look at that shape, drew his gun and emptied its barrel in its chest.

A tremor passed over Reba's body. For one moment longer it stood erect. Then the parody of what had been Reba Loveless collapsed in a heap of decaying flesh and bones. As it fell, Barndollar thought he saw something run out of the dead mouth—"like a big curly-haired mole, or a kind of shaggy spider," as he described it later. It was making a chuckling noise as it scuttled across the floor and out the door into the warm darkness. Joe hurled his empty gun after it, but missed. He dashed out after it, only to see it disappear in the grass. Although there was a rustling in the mock-orange hedge that bordered Yancey's Meadow, he could see nothing.

The body of Jeff's first wife lay where it had fallen, in a gruesome little pile. The imitation life that had supported it briefly, that had raised it from the grave and had kept it hidden in the abandoned well until its moment had come to present itself to Dorothy—that life had gone with its alien guest.

BUT Aline's still-living body moved feebly, and Jeff was down on his knees, his brain whirling while his hands helped her to sit up. Her hands moved feebly at her mauled throat. As remembrance of the horror flooded back she began to cry silently, with long shuddering sobs. Then she saw Dorothy.

Her stepdaughter stood like a small statue, her eyes round with fright, but no sound, other than that first faint gasp, had come from her.

"Dorothy...Harry Todd?" Aline managed to say.

"They're all right, Darling—don't try to talk," Jeff cried, while the boy threw himself upon her, sobbing, "Don't die, Aline! Don't die!"

Aline still looked at the little girl. She had such a queer, frozen appearance...

"Dorothy?" she said again. Dorothy wanted to answer, wanted to cry out as her brother had, "Don't die, Aline—Mother!" She wanted to say many things to the woman she had resented for so long—like, "I know I was bad...I wanted you to go away and for Mommy to come back...but I didn't want all *this!* I didn't want Mommy like *that*...and I'm sorry for what I did to Mudge...and oh, Mother, I'm scared! I'm scared!"

But nothing of this would come out. Her throat felt funny and she couldn't make the words sound like they ought to—only a kind of choked gurgle.

Jeff's jaw dropped. "My God, she can't talk! Aline! Dolly—she can't *talk!* Oh, my poor baby!" And Jeff suddenly knew that the horror had been too much for one small girl to face, as she had, alone, in a dark room, and that it had struck her dumb.

Yet, as the deputy dialed Doctor Oldham with a shaking hand, a faint, half-bitter hope crept into Aline's mind. She'll need me now, she thought. Until the fountains of her speech can be unlocked again, Dolly will need me now.

FARTHER and farther away, over the darkling fields in and out among the misty trees, along the reedy banks of creeks and down into damp hollows, the thing that the children had called Old Mop-Head hurried and danced and tumbled.

It felt light and gay, but its strength was fading. The fierce but transient power, which had filled its makeshift body, which had spurred it to burrow and rip and choke and reanimate, was leaving it. Its essential being had not been harmed by the bullets, but its ramshackle body was coming apart. Here fell away a giant mandible, there a long shred of borrowed possum-fur, there again a beetle's wing and a spider's leg. It was getting sleepy, too. It wanted to find a place that was deep and dark and hidden, and wet with an ancient wetness, where it could rest until it had assembled a new shape. This world it had stumbled into had all sorts of exciting possibilities, all kinds of shapes, and materials for shapes, and other beings to talk to and do things for and make friends of!

But right now all it wanted was to sleep and sleep…

It began to look about for a forgotten cistern or an old well.

THE END

THE GHOST THAT NEVER DIED

By Elizabeth Sheldon

...done to death by the ghost of a person who was still alive.

I SUPPOSE few people will believe the story of Miriam Tromley's death and its sequel, even today. That is why I had never told of the strange things I had seen, either at the inquest or afterward. I might have confessed it to the police, shrieked it aloud on Broadway. Who would have believed me then? But the time is not far off when the world will know that such things can be.

I was Evelyn's stenographer for three years. It was a queer job. I guess old Parton, whose name adorned the title page of the magazine, hardly knew how he came to be an editor. It had started as a sort of advertisement bulletin for his cereals and tinned food; then Miriam Tromley came to be his secretary. She had been an editor on a woman's magazine. She was a nervous little woman with all sorts of half-baked talents, and the first thing old Parton knew she had turned his biscuit literature into a magazine.

The magazine—*Mother and Child*, you must remember it— grew larger and thicker until it needed another worker in the editorial department. Miriam Tromley had a friend who, according to her own tale, was in the hardest kind of ill-luck at the time, and she convinced stingy old Parton that *Mother and Child* needed her afflicted friend's services. That friend was Evelyn Renard. This all happened about a year before they took me on. When I arrived on the scene, Evelyn had been promoted from assistant to co-editor. When I went in answer to their advertisement for a stenographer it was Evelyn Renard who interviewed me. I remember so well my first impression of her. She appeared to have risen hastily as I entered, and stood at her

THE GHOST THAT NEVER DIED

BY ELIZABETH SHELDON
Heading by Vincent Napoli

desk ill at ease, although I was only a prospective stenographer. I felt as if she had hurriedly concealed something as I entered. I do not mean this literally, it was just the impression of something furtive about the woman herself. When you were in the room with her she did not look at you, she watched you like an animal ready to anticipate the movement of its enemy. I always felt something reptilian about her, and strange to say, she had a liking for snakes instead of the repulsion most of us feel for them.

I always felt sorry for Miriam Tromley. She lacked repose, a frail, faded little woman, neither young nor old. She knew twice as much as her co-editor, but she lacked assurance; whereas Evelyn Renard was a raw, shameless and brilliant faker. No one knew anything about her antecedents. She laid claim to a millionaire French-Canadian father who had lost his money in disastrous speculations.

She engaged me at an unusually small salary, but I was not in a position to be particular just then. I afterward learned that Evelyn had done some very efficient work reducing the salaries of the entire staff after her promotion, although she always attributed this policy to some hardhearted power above her.

For a time I lost sight of my first disagreeable impression of her, for Evelyn, as I have said, was friendly with all the office employees, and she told such pathetic stories about herself that everyone pitied her. Even hard old Parton made her work as easy as possible, while Miriam Tromley, who had an income of her own, was always responding to some dire need of Evelyn's, and incidentally spent hours doing Evelyn's work—for which she received scant thanks.

OLD PARTON had had rather a fancy for Miriam Tromley at the start. At the time Evelyn appeared upon the scene, Miss Sampson says, they all thought he would marry her, but after Evelyn came Miriam's influence declined. She made him believe that Miriam was inefficient. It did not come about too quickly. Miriam never suspected, but no one else was much surprised when Evelyn Renard was put over her. Evelyn was then editor-in-chief. When that happened we could all prophesy the next step, which would, of course, be the total exit of Miriam.

We all knew it but Miriam. She seemed restless and a little anxious at times, but whatever she may have feared she was never suspicious of Evelyn. By that time I had begun to lose my sympathy with our afflicted employer; I had seen too much of the inner working of her office politics.

"She'll make a grand political boss when women really get their teeth into politics," said Miss Sampson the day we uncovered the maternity corset graft that was going on the woman's page.

ONE day when Miss Renard was ill I went to her apartment to take some dictation, and afterward she got talking. She said she was lonely. I think she was afraid to be alone. Anyway, she indulged in some of the wildest flights of fancy I ever heard from a sane person.

"One day, Miss Morton," she said, "I went into my room and saw myself lying on the bed. Now what do you think of that?"

I thought at the time, "My dear Madam, I'd hate to tell you what I think of it!" And I remembered my first impression—that there was something uncanny about Evelyn Renard. Also, I don't believe she ever had an idea in her life. I don't think she wanted to have one. She preferred to use her neighbor's. Evelyn liked the idea of having other people do her work for her.

When the exposure of the maternity corset graft came, of course Evelyn contrived to keep her skirts clear of it. I don't know how much old Parton was on to the mechanism of it, but I was wise to it from the beginning, and I don't believe Evelyn ever knew that I knew. If she did, what a fool she must have thought me not to have blackmailed her out of a good income with my knowledge! That is what she would have done in my place.

Occasionally I used to catch glimpses of Miriam Tromley looking worried and anchorless, coming in and out of the office. She had not been able to get another position. She used to come in to see Evelyn at times when she knew old Parton would be out. Evelyn had succeeded in making a complete breach between them. At the same time she sympathized ardently with Miriam for the injustice that had been done her.

"Men are like that," I heard her say one day in accents of bitter sympathy to Miriam. "The more you do for them the more they expect. You poor dear! You worked yourself to death for old Parton and this is what you get for it."

I HAVE never known just the nature of the next crooked deal that Evelyn put over. It was an opportunity that came to her in some way through the office. Some dishonorable use that she made of inside information. She covered her tracks to the end. The trouble came because she began to be afraid that Miriam knew about it, and as a result to be haunted by the fear of exposure.

Miriam had come in one day while Evelyn was having a conference with an advertising man. She was obliged to go with the man into another office, leaving Miriam alone beside her desk with her papers spread out on top of it.

I think that was the beginning of her suspicion that Miriam knew what she was up to, although I knew that Miss Tromley was incapable of reading other people's letters. From that day on I could see that Evelyn was afraid of Miriam. Later I knew that she hated her. I imagine that people like Evelyn Renard always hate those who have given them their start, especially when they have done their benefactor an injury in return.

Of course there was something in those papers that Evelyn had reason to be very nervous about. I had known for some time that she had papers, which she kept, locked up as if she were in the secret service.

ONE afternoon after leaving the office I found that I had left behind a pile of manuscripts I had to read, and I went back to get them.

As I opened the door of Miss Renard's office I distinctly saw her at her desk drawing out a paper from a drawer that she always kept locked.

"Why, Miss Renard, I thought you had left long ago!" I exclaimed. As I walked in I knocked against a pile of books and papers on the corner of a desk and they began to fall to the floor. I bent to pick them up, and when I rose again—about the space of two seconds—Miss Renard was gone. She must have slipped out the other door, but how she managed it so noiselessly I don't know.

I told her about it the next day, and while I was telling it I noticed a curious sort of glitter in her eyes—snake-like I called it to myself. She dismissed me and my anecdote a little shortly.

"You were day-dreaming, Miss Morton; I was in a suburban train on my way to Rye at that time yesterday, and asleep at that. I nearly went past my station."

As it happened I had proof afterward that she had told me the truth, for Miss Sampson who lives in Mt. Vernon was on the same train, but all the same I felt sure that Evelyn Renard was living some sort of a double life, for I saw some queer goings on in those days.

For one thing I felt sure that she "shadowed" Miriam Tromley. Miriam had finally found an advertising position of some sort, and did not come in so often. When she did, Evelyn's dread was most apparent. There was certainly something that she was terribly afraid to have Miriam find out. Twice after dark I saw her following Miriam, always at a little distance behind her, and walking more noiselessly than you would believe a human being could walk.

One day when Miriam had left the office I caught Evelyn looking after her with an expression that actually made me shiver. She must have noticed the look on my face, for she quietly rearranged her features and said with the sweetest tone of false sympathy—one I had come to know so well:

"Dear Miss Tromley is not looking so well. Haven't you noticed it? I am really troubled about her."

I muttered that I hadn't noticed it especially, and as our eyes met I knew with a sense of chill along my spine, that the editor of *Mother and Child* wished that her former benefactor was dead.

The next day I overheard part of a conversation between them that seemed rather to give reality to Evelyn's fears, which I had taken to be just the imaginary alarms of a guilty conscience.

"You are making a mistake, Evelyn," I heard Miriam say, "and if I can't make you see it I will have to take some other means of stopping it."

Then Evelyn's voice, rasping and hard, "Go ahead—I don't care! You needn't think that you can down me—"

That was all I heard, but enough to know that Miriam seemed to be threatening some sort of exposure, and that Evelyn's mood was determined and defiant.

I did not know what it was about then. Afterward I was able to make a shrewd guess.

THE next day was the strangest in my life. Afterward I wondered if I had lost my reason temporarily, if I had suffered from delusions, but now I understand…I will tell it exactly as it happened.

In the first place it leaked out—as such things usually do—that Evelyn had hooked old Parton. They were to be married quietly the next day. It had long been a betting proposition in the office, with the odds on Evelyn's side. At least all the women except the new flapper stenog had bet on her.

Just before five o'clock, Miriam called to see Evelyn and was refused. The editor's door was closed to all visitors. Something in the make-up had to be changed at the last minute, and Evelyn had ordered her dinner sent in. She was going to work until she was through, she said, and short of a bomb explosion or a fire in the building—so she instructed the night operator—no one was to knock on her door.

As I stood inside the street entrance pursuing an elusive dime in the depths of my bag, I caught sight of the dismissed Miriam hanging indecisively on the outskirts of the hurrying crowd. I remembered afterward her bewildered disconsolate expression and, what I had not realized before, the peculiar indecision, the marked weakness of the face. It occurred to me that she had in some way depended upon Evelyn's hard selfish strength, and that without her she was rudderless, like a lost dog without its master.

Just as I had captured my dime and started to go, the elevator came down and I saw Evelyn—supposedly locked up in her office at work, slip out and pass silently out to the street.

It did not surprise me. I think I always expected Evelyn to have some different purpose from the one she openly owned up to, and I should have thought nothing of it if it had not been for Miriam's strange treatment of her.

Evelyn walked directly up to Miriam, but Miriam simply stared straight into her face and walked past as if she were not there at all. I don't mean that Miriam cut her, but that she looked—or seemed to look—directly at the spot where Evelyn stood without seeing her. Certainly Miriam must be in some disturbed state of mind for such absent-mindedness to be possible when faced by the very person she had come to see!

Miriam turned toward Fifth Avenue; Evelyn followed at a short distance and, my curiosity and apprehension now thoroughly awake, I followed them both.

Evelyn did not make any effort to overtake Miriam. She slipped quietly after her through the crowd in an eel-like way she had, so close behind I marveled that Miriam never once saw her. She did seem to have some sense of being followed. Twice she turned and looked back, but (I remembered afterward) although the second time she caught sight of me and bowed, she never once saw Evelyn.

I followed them all the way to Miriam's apartment in Greenwich Village. She lived in a sort of studio building, an old house with dark winding halls. And never once during that strange walk did Miriam discover that Evelyn was following her. Never once did Evelyn discover me!

At the door of her apartment Miriam paused to let herself in, while Evelyn drew back into the shadow.

I waited farther back, near the stairs. It was not long before Miriam came out again—to go to her dinner perhaps, or to get something to cook at home. I saw Evelyn creep nearer. There was only a dim gas-jet burning far down the hall; otherwise the place was almost dark.

As Miriam stood in the doorway of her room, a pathetic little silhouette against the light, at last Evelyn went openly up to her and spoke. At least I thought she spoke, although I heard no sound. Miriam turned to look at her vaguely…without surprise. Evelyn seemed to be urging her to do something, and Miriam listened with her eyes cast down like one in thought, but she did not answer.

After a moment she turned back into her room, and noiselessly Evelyn slipped through the door after her, close on her heels.

They left it open. I stood on the threshold of Miriam's apartment uneasy and irresolute, watching them. Still without speaking, Miriam went to the bathroom, turned on the light, took a small bottle from the medicine cabinet and picked up a glass, while silent Evelyn watched. I could see it all from where I stood. And still neither of them spoke, only the place seemed filled with the electric pulsations of Evelyn's will.

I saw Miriam pour the contents of the vial into a glass; then for a moment she seemed to hesitate, and in that interval Miriam seemed to grow vague and weak, while Evelyn became strong, tall, terrific… She was advising Miriam, but it was advice that was more like a threat or a command. Even then I did not suspect. How could I have understood? I knew nothing of these things then…not until Miriam raised the glass to her lips—not until it fell from her nerveless fingers, and I saw her turn with a dazed face half falling into a chair, did I realize what the glass must have contained...

She saw me then, she called my name. I jumped forward just in time to save her from falling, then turned to Evelyn just as she was escaping from the room. I sprang after her and caught her wrist, but it slipped from my grasp...something cool and light...not solid...yet cold, with a curious indescribable cold-ness... For a long time I could feel the sensation of it, like men-thol on my hand. Then I bent over Miriam—she was totally unconscious.

I found an art student in a neighboring studio. We got the poor girl into her bed and telephoned for a doctor, but he was too late. It was cyanide, and death had been instantaneous.

AND now I come to the strangest part of my story. After I got home that night about nine o'clock, I rang up Miss Wharton, Mr. Parton's secretary, to tell her of poor Miriam Tromley's death, and learned that she had gone back to Evelyn's apartment that night at eight o'clock—old Parton had sent her—because he could get no answer from her telephone—and found her in bed in charge of a trained nurse! The doctor had just left. It seemed that Evelyn had had some sort of a seizure while working alone in her office. Miss Wharton (who had not been employed in the office very long) found the case most pathetic.

"No one knows how long she had lain there unconscious, poor soul, all alone, with no one to come to her help! The watchman found her lying beside her desk. He noticed the light and went to investigate."

"The night watchman!" I repeated. "Do you know what time it was?"

"No, it wasn't the night watchman, it was James. He found her just before he left, and he leaves, doesn't he, at half-past six?"

Half-past six? The very hour of Miriam Tromley's death. For by a curious impulse I had glanced at my wristwatch when the doctor had dropped Miriam's hand and pronounced her dead.

According to that, Evelyn Renard was in her own office at the very moment I had seen her leave Miriam Tromley's apartment forty blocks away!

Almost beside myself, I hung up the receiver without bidding Miss Wharton good-bye and went straight to Evelyn Renard's house and asked for the nurse. She looked a little curious when she saw my face. I think she thought that I was Evelyn's next of kin in a state of distraction.

"I can't imagine what brought on Miss Renard's attack," she said. "She seemed to be in a sort of trance when they found her. She must have been dead set on something, for her face was fixed with the look of a man in a death grip. It was awful to see that look on her white unconscious face. Seemed like she must have been making some big mental drive and just dropped off after it like that."

"They found her about half-past six?" I asked.

The nurse stared as if she found my question odd.

"So I understand," she said and returned to her patient. I could hear her moaning faintly—rather a dreadful sound.

It was a fact then, Evelyn had been in her own office in a fainting-fit at the very hour when I had seen her urging Miriam Tromley to take her own life!

THE marriage was postponed for a time. Three days later Evelyn came back to the office. She went about looking so white and appealing that even the publicity manager pitied her.

"Poor girl, how she feels her friend's death!" he said.

I never told what I had seen. How could I have told it in the face of the facts? With her own hand Miriam Tromley had lifted the glass of poison to her lips. Had I not seen her in the very act?

About a month afterward Evelyn had what the doctors called a nervous breakdown—a breakdown with delusions. She told me one of them a few days before they took her away to the sanitarium. We were alone in the office.

I had just said to her, "You really ought to take a rest, Miss Renard. You are just keeping up on will-power."

And she had answered, "Perhaps I am. It is wonderful what one's will can do." She bent toward me like one telling a secret. "Did you know that you can make your will do things at a distance when you are asleep?"

"What do you mean?" I asked, controlling my impulse to draw back from her.

She leaned nearer with a look I didn't like to meet in her murky eyes. "Why, don't you know? You can go to bed at night and set your will to do something you want to accomplish—miles away—and it will do the thing for you, just as if you were there. Sometimes you can half remember it afterward...like a dream."

I remembered that conversation afterward...when old Parton died.

Evelyn did not stay long in the sanitarium. In two weeks she was back in the office completely restored.

Miriam Tromley had not been dead a month when Evelyn Renard became Evelyn Parton. Summer was approaching. Of course she gave up her job at the office—although she playfully remarked, she should always keep an eye on it—and she did.

Mr. and Mrs. Parton sailed on the newest highest-priced steamer for Europe in June. That was the last we ever saw of old Parton. He died suddenly in an obscure town in Italy, leaving Evelyn his sole heir. She was now sole owner of the business, not to speak of all that it had made.

I feel dreadfully about old Parton's death. How can I do otherwise? If I had told what I had seen it might have saved his life.

He had walked off an upper balcony in his sleep, so they told us... But who had urged him out there...a useless old encumbrance now that his will was made and his fortune safely within Evelyn's grasp?

I can see a dark shadowy figure behind poor old Parton, softly urging him over the brink, a spirit you might call it, a ghost that never died. "Ghosts of the living," the Japanese call them, the soul sent out in sleep. Is not sleep Death's Sister? Evelyn had concentrated upon Miriam's death, willing her to self-destruction. Sometimes it is known as astral murder.

It would appear to be the perfect crime, wouldn't it, evidence upon which no jury would convict? But Evelyn's career did not end with Miriam Tromley, or even with old Parton.

IT SEEMED for a time as if nothing could stop Evelyn. Strange that little Blanche O'Hara should have been the one.

Blanche was MacDonough's private secretary. MacDonough was our business manager and a very keen man. I am sure he never cared for Evelyn, although of course he was far from guessing what she really was. He was fond of Blanche, whether fond enough to marry her one couldn't tell, but at least his favor made Blanche a person of some consequence, and Evelyn had always feared discovery—strange mixture that she was of iron will and cowardice.

She never dreamed that I suspected her—luckily for me—or I should have gone the way of poor Miriam and old Parton. But for some reason her apprehensions and suspicions fastened upon Blanche. Evelyn more or less took charge of the business after old Parton died. She never had an office in the building, but at least once in the day she would drop in on us—of course at the time she thought she was least expected; and quite often if MacDonough was out, or really busy, this brought her in touch with Blanche.

I don't believe Blanche had the faintest suspicion of what Evelyn was like. She was a frank, straightforward child, with great, clear, rather light blue eyes. Though light, they were very striking, because her eyelashes were long, and dark like her hair. They were rather uncanny eyes, and she had a way of fixing them upon you and leaving them there. She was probably thinking of something else when she did it, most likely MacDonough, but she certainly made you feel as if she was reading your innermost thoughts, piercing your very soul. It would have been a hard thing to lie to Blanche. I could see that her eyes got on Evelyn's nerves. She would do anything rather than meet them.

Blanche was a good kid, clean straight through. Like the heroine in the old-fashioned melodrama, she was the sole support of a widowed mother. But she was not sentimental about it, never made capital out of it, or regretted the necessity to go without little feminine vanities because of it.

It seems that I was predestined to the role of onlooker, for I was the sole witness of that momentous last meeting between Evelyn and Blanche.

It was one of those warmish days in winter when New York offices seem unbearably hot. Evelyn had dropped in at noon when she knew MacDonough would be out. That made me curious to start with, because I knew it meant that this time, instead of avoiding, she wanted to see Blanche. MacDonough did quite a bit of business at luncheon, and consequently was often absent for a long time at that hour. While he was out Blanche was obliged to be in. Of course Evelyn knew that.

The first thing Evelyn did when she entered was to ask to have the window wide open. It was I who had ushered her in, and I remained near the doorway frankly watching. For some reason Evelyn thought me of no account. She never seemed to notice my comings or goings.

Blanche went to the window and threw it all the way up. Evelyn stole up behind her like a shadow. She never seemed to walk so that we heard her, and she almost always dressed in black. Evelyn leaned against the right-hand side of the window ledge, Blanche was at the left.

"What a perfectly gorgeous day!" Blanche said, and leaned out, drawing in long breaths. "What a view from this window!"

Evelyn answered. "Why, all those buildings are on Long Island! I wonder what that tall tower is."

She pointed to something real or imaginary so far to the north that Blanche had to lean quite far out to see it. The window ledge was rather low, and it made me nervous to see Blanche do it. I don't know what it was that suddenly made me look from Blanche to Evelyn.

No, Evelyn had no intention of pushing her out, not with her hands. But if you could have seen her eyes! Never so long as I live shall I forget them—a snake's eyes sending out live fires of hatred—hatred and something else...

I knew what it was. It was the thing that must be in a snake's eyes when it is charming the dove to its death.

Farther and farther little Blanche leaned out; a scream rose to my lips, I made a dart forward; then, sharply, Blanche drew in and turned her eyes upon Evelyn. And under her eyes Evelyn seemed to shrink and withdraw within herself, as if like the demon in a fairy story she was going to vanish. But she did not vanish. She stood staring, staring at Blanche, straight into those wide, clear, pure blue eyes.

It was the strangest thing I have ever seen. From her evil murky eyes Evelyn was sending out something, something that was a veritable missile of death, sending it straight into Blanche's eyes. For a moment she was able to send it as a writhing snake may spit out venom in its last hour. But the thing that she sent could not reach its victim. From that clear light it rebounded back to its source, straight into the evil soul that lay behind Evelyn's dark eyes. A boomerang!

She made a wild movement like a creature shot. Blanche screamed; for a second, a dark thing outflung against the sky...then silence. Twenty stories below, Evelyn Parton lay on the sidewalk, broken beyond recognition in the midst of the wild panic of the passers-by.

Miriam Tromley was timid and neurotic, Parton was a feeble old man. But Blanche, young, strong, clean of soul, was not vulnerable to Evelyn's evil power, which, deflected from its target, rebounded upon her who sent it, forcing her to the suicidal act she had tried to will Blanche to perform.

When MacDonough married Blanche he took new offices in another building, for never afterward could Blanche bear to go in that room. I think little as she sensed what had happened there, she did realize that she had been very close to the great force of Evil in that place.

THE END

BIRTH OF A MONSTER

By Richard Stark
(aka Donald E. Westlake)

Those ghastly ghouls that have escaped the grave by feeding on a diet of blood from the living are the deadly enemies of all mankind, the unholy vampires...

HE was sound asleep when the phone rang. He woke up, suddenly and completely, between the first and second rings, and lay with his eyes open, staring at the ceiling above him in the darkness, wondering why he had awakened.

The phone jangled again. Reaching out, he fumbled for the chain on the lamp beside his bed, found it, blinked at the sudden yellow light. The alarm clock said just past two thirty. By the third ring, he was sitting beside the bed, pawing with his toes for his slippers.

He left the bedroom, walked down the dark hall toward the dining room, promising himself yet again that he would definitely see about having an extension phone put in the bedroom. After all, a doctor, general practitioner—although it had been over three months since he had last been called so late. An emergency, that time. A drunken husband, a long, narrow flight of stairs—four bones broken and an hysterical wife.

He wondered what it would be this time. As the fourth ring began, he picked up the phone, said, "Doctor Lamming."

It was a man's voice. He didn't sound at all excited. "Doctor, my wife is about to have a baby. There's no time to get to the hospital. I have no car. If you could come—"

He didn't recognize the voice, couldn't remember any pregnancies due for two or three weeks yet. He said, "Is your wife one of my patients?"

There was a pause, then, "No," said the voice. "We just moved in, we're new in town. Can you come?"

"Certainly. What's the address?"

"Four fifty two Larchmont. At the top of the hill."

"The old estate?"

"Yes. We've just moved in."

"I'll be there in half an hour. Maybe less."

"Thank you, doctor."

He hung up, hurried back to the bedroom and dressed. He knew the estate, at the end of Larchmont Road. Empty for years. He hadn't known anyone had moved in. Who would want to move in there? Artists, perhaps. Thinking the place was "quaint." Probably planning to renovate, modernize, surprise their friends from the city. More and more commuters were moving into town, and a lot of them had strange tastes.

The office was in the front of the house. He stopped and loaded the bag, hurried out, leaving the cabinet doors open in the dark house behind him.

His car was in the garage. He climbed in, backed out to the street, left the garage open and hurried across town.

Larchmont Drive was a long, winding road, flanked by old gabled structures and new ranch-style one-story homes, the meeting of old and new, the locals and the commuters. The road wound and wiggled its way up the hill, ending at the great closed gates to the estate. If the estate had once had a name, once been associated with one particular owner, the name was now lost and forgotten. The brooding building at the top of the hill was now known only as "the estate." Not even a capital letter. It didn't even attract children, it didn't even have a reputation for being haunted. It was only a lonely and empty shell, stuck away on the top of the hill. Its walls were gray-black from lack of paint, its front windows, facing west, shone orange in the late afternoon, but were dull black the rest of the time.

Doctor Lamming drove up the road, noticing that the huge wrought-iron gates were open now, for the first time in his memory. He drove through and on up the curving, pitted road to the estate.

There was no light. He got out of the car, holding his leather bag, and looked at the place, wondering if this call were only some practical joker's impractical idea of a joke. Then he saw a light moving within the house, and the heavy front door whined open.

There was a man there; holding in his hand a kerosene lamp. He said, "Doctor Lamming?"

"Yes. Coming." He trotted up the warped steps and across the rail-less pillared verandah to the door.

THE man was short and thin and sallow. He might have been thirty, or forty, or fifty. His hair was black and straight and rather long, and his face was long and thin, with prominent cheekbones, deep-set eyes and thin, bloodless lips. The thin lips smiled slightly and he said, "We just moved in. No electricity as yet."

"Water?"

"Yes. We have our own well. My wife is upstairs."

It was the first time Doctor Lamming had ever been inside the building. The weak kerosene lamp showed very little, but he caught glimpses, as they moved down the wide central hall to the staircase, of high-ceilinged, barren rooms, of occasional pieces of ancient, dust-covered, sheet-draped furniture, of curtainless windows and silence and emptiness.

The other man said, "Our furniture hasn't come yet. Most of it. Just enough for the one bedroom."

Doctor Lamming noticed, now, a faint, undecipherable accent in the other man's speech. He couldn't quite place it. He said, "By the way. I don't know your name."

The other stopped at the foot of the staircase and turned, his right hand extended. "I'm terribly sorry, Doctor. I'm not thinking straight. Cargill is my name. Anton Cargill."

They shook hands, and Doctor Lamming was surprised at the coldness and thinness of Cargill's hand. And, too, though Cargill claimed he wasn't thinking straight, though he claimed his wife was upstairs, about to give birth, the man's voice and manner and tone were completely blank, completely unemotional.

Cargill turned away and climbed the stairs to the second floor, the doctor behind him. At thirty-two, with six years of general practice behind him, Doctor Lamming considered himself reasonably used to the vagaries and variety of human beings, but this complete lack of emotion from an expectant father was something new. He said, "Your first child, Mr. Cargill?"

They had reached the top of the stairs, and Cargill led the way to the left. "Yes," he said. "As a matter of fact, it came as something of a surprise. We had been under the impression that it was—impossible for us."

"It sometimes takes a while," said the doctor.

Cargill walked into the bedroom, and the doctor followed. There were already three kerosene lamps in the room. The furniture was old-fashioned, massive-looking, chests and dressers and chairs and, in the center of the room, a huge canopy bed. The woman lay on the bed, her eyes closed, her black hair spread out against the pillow, her face as pale and white as her husband's in the light of the lamps. The doctor put his bag down on the table beside the bed, and the woman groaned, moving her head.

Cargill stood beside the bed, looking without expression at his wife. "Soon now, I think," he said.

"Yes," said the doctor. "If you would—towels, hot water. Lots of both."

"Of course," said Cargill.

Taking one of the lamps, he left the room.

The woman on the bed was undoubtedly in labor. She groaned again, and murmured, but Doctor Lamming couldn't make out what she had said. He stripped the blanket away, and saw that Cargill had been right. Soon now. He took his tools from the bag, wrapped in a towel and spread them out on a table. His own stainless steel equipment and the two silver scalpels that had been his father's, which he now carried more as good luck charms than anything else. Memories of his father, who had been the Doctor Lamming in the town before him, and in whose footsteps he had striven to walk.

The woman was in pain. He worked rapidly, not noticing the odd, the strange, the unbelievable, not noticing anything but the work he was doing. The baby didn't seem to want to be born. It was difficult, it was long and exhausting, but finally he held the infant in his hands. The child breathed, it weakly moved its chubby fists, but it did not cry out.

He set the child down and stared. He had been working with such absorption, had been so blind to everything aside from his own movements and the movements of the child, that now he could do nothing but stare, with shock and disbelief.

It had been a bloodless birth. A birth completely without blood. And now, as he stared with horror at the woman's face, her eyes closed and her mouth open as she lay in exhausted sleep, he knew what this woman was. He looked at the sharp, pointed teeth, the long, fang-like canines, the pale lips, the chalk-white face and he knew just what she was.

And what he had to do. The furniture in the room was old, some of it was beaten and rickety. He grabbed a chair, wrenched at it, managed to pull one of the slats out of the back. He reached for a knife, one of the delicate instruments of his profession, he hacked at the slat of wood until one end of it was sharp and pointed. Turning, he closed his eyes and plunged the wooden stake into the sleeping woman's heart.

She moved, with a sudden lurching spasm, her cold arms beating against his face, and from her throat came the scream of the banshee, the scream of the doomed in Hell. He fell away from her, lost his balance, toppled to the floor. Rising, he saw that she was still, and that she was incredibly old.

He had to get away. He turned to the door, and Cargill was standing there, in one hand the kerosene lamp, in the other a handful of folded towels.

They stared at each other, and Cargill's eyes seemed to be alight with passion, with rage, with obscene lust.

Doctor Lamming backed away, bumping into the table on which lay his bag and his tools. He stared at the other with loathing and fear. "Vampire!" he screamed, and his voice echoed through the empty rooms of the house.

Cargill set down the lamp, dropped the towels on the floor. "Yes," he said. "A new world. *Our* new world, too. You'll never know how difficult it was to make the crossing. To a new world, where we are not hunted, where we are not known, where we are safe."

"You are known," the doctor told him. "You are not safe."

"Known only as legend." Cargill looked without emotion at the bed. "You have killed my wife," he said. "But I will have a new wife. And first I will have a new brother."

The doctor backed away again, around the table, clutching at the bag on the table, wondering if he could hurl the bag, duck, run around the man—the vampire—the *thing* before him, down the stairs, to safety.

"The gates are closed," Cargill told him. "You are mine." And his arms moved up, above his head. But, no, his arms were stretched out, toward the doctor, and he rose, to the beat of dusty black wings, to swoop down upon the doctor.

The doctor screamed and pawed at the table. His father's scalpels! His hand touched one of them, and he brought it up, a glinting silver blade, and as the hungry mouth lunged down at him he pushed the blade deep into the other's neck.

Cargill slumped before him, clutching the doctor's coat, gasping oaths in a language the doctor had never before heard, and the doctor swung once more with the silver scalpel, driving it deep into Cargill's chest. Cargill screamed, and the monstrous wings fluttered, and the vampire lay dead.

Doctor Lamming staggered from the room. He had to get away, he had to get help, he had to call the police, there might be more of them here, more of them. In the darkness, without the lamp to guide him, he stumbled and ran along the upper hall, clattered and lurched and half-fell down the broad staircase, ran panting to the front door and to his car.

The car started at the first try. He turned it around, backing, turning, then pressed the accelerator to the floor and the car leaped ahead, to race around the curving driveway to the road.

The gates were closed, as Cargill had said. He hit the brakes, shoving down with his foot, and the car squealed and swerved to a stop inches from the gates. He got out and ran to the gates, pushed on them, and they started to open.

Something brushed his face. He turned and looked up, and it hovered just above him, its tiny dusky wings beating silently, and then it plunged and Doctor Lamming screamed his life away.

The baby.

THE END

WAY STATION

By Mary Elizabeth Counselman

Perhaps the young people hadn't read carefully enough the sign over the door.

RAIN whipped at the little car, plastering sheets of water against the windshield faster than the wipers could fan it clear. The man at the wheel, crouched forward to peer through the blinding storm, ran a palm quickly over the misted glass; then smiled and patted the knee of the girl pressed close to his side.

"Honey—we can't go on in this downpour. Better pull off the highway, at least until I can see three feet ahead! ...Cold?" he inquired tenderly, as the slender body shivered against him.

The girl shook her head. "Just...nervous, I guess," she smiled back, with a studied attempt at gayety. "After all, this is my first honeymoon!"

"Some honeymoon!" The bridegroom, a tall stocky young man, whose army uniform contrasted grimly with his bride's frilly suit and flower-hat—laughed wryly. "For so long I've been dreaming of this, slogging around in the rain in Korea... A furlough! Ah-h! We'd spend a wonderful, sunny week together in a musical-comedy setting! And what do I get?" He chuckled, "More rain! Besides," he added sheepishly, "I think I took a wrong turn back there someplace. Can't see any road-- signs in all this..."

He broke off, slowing the car at sight of a byroad at right angles to the paved highway ahead. Pulling off into it, he discovered it to be the entrance of a gravel driveway, ill kept and deeply pitted with holes. As the car jolted to a standstill, deluged by a fresh downpour, a huge truck rumbled past— dangerously close as it hugged the edge of the pavement. The young soldier whistled; tipped back his cap; mopped his face.

Illustration by H. W. Silvey

"Whew! That was *close!* Can't tell when those trailers will sideswipe you on a wet road…"

"Like a dinosaur's tail?" His bride giggled, snuggling against him. "I wasn't worried, Tom. Not with you driving."

The boy grinned, and held her close for a moment. "No? I'm glad you have such confidence in me. Wish *I* had as much! And knew where the merry hell we are!"

HE ROLLED down a window glass. Rain lashed at him as he peered out, straining his eyes through the storm-hastened twilight. With a movable search-lamp he swept a yellow arc of brilliance, like a finger pushing at the curtain of rain. It halted abruptly.

"Hey! Some kind of sign up there on a post…*FARADAY HOUSE,*" he read with difficulty. *"Miss Adelaide Faraday, Prop. Overnight…"* A grin curved his anxious mouth. "Well! How about that for luck? It's a tourist home!" The finger of light probed deeper into the rain, seeking out a dim white blur at the end of the gravel drive. "Doesn't look too bad. One of those old Gone-with-the-wind jobs. White-columned veranda, fanlight over the door. They probably serve wonderful meals; fried chicken and biscuits. How about it, Jean baby? Take a look…"

The girl was looking—not at the storm-blurred house, but at her husband's earnest expression.

"Anyplace," she whispered. "Any place at all, darling. So long as we can be together, even for…a little while," her eyes misted over suddenly, like the rainy windshield, traveling from the boy's eager young face to the chevrons on his khaki sleeve. "A week! Just a *week…*"

THE shadow of fear rose between them abruptly at her words, the dark fear of all lovers—that of being separated, of being torn apart by forces stronger than the love that bound them together. The boy reached out, snatched his young bride into his embrace, and held her tight. She clung to him, sobbing.

"Oh, Tommy! If only you didn't have to go back! So...so *soon!*"

"Hey, now! We promised to pretend. Remember?" His voice as he tried to comfort her was unsteady, but determinedly light.

"Time is relative," he chanted the familiar ritual. "A day can be 24 hours—or a minute. Or *ten years!* We have seven days, huh? Seven times ten are seventy. ...Why, we've already been married—let's see—fifteen years! Wednesday will be our Golden Anniversary! And by Friday, when I have to...to...say, how long can a guy *stand* being married to one old hag?"

The sobbing against his shoulder ceased. With a forlorn but game little sniff, the bride sat up and managed a wavery grin.

"Okay..." As the rain slacked briefly, she peered out, following the pointing finger of the searchlight. "It...it looks kind of...old and rundown. Maybe they won't charge as much as a motel," she added practically, "and we can have more to spend in Florida!"

"Women!" The bridegroom hooted, steering the car up the driveway. "Right in the middle of a tender love-scene, they start worrying about the budget! Can't you dames...ever...?"

His voice trailed as the car, following the curve of the gravel drive, came to a halt in front of the big white house they had dimly glimpsed through the rain. On closer inspection, it was very badly in need of repair. Paint curled on the heavy fluted columns, one of which slanted at a dangerous angle. The fanlight over the door looked like a grinning mouth with several teeth out, and the ornate brass knocker was tarnished black; so black that the young couple could barely make out the name engraved on it: FARADAY. Somewhere a shutter creaked on a rusty hinge, with a sound like a groan of pain. Yet, in front of the door, a shabby *Welcome* mat gave a contrasting note of hospitality.

Drenched, shivering, the newlyweds hesitated on the wide veranda. They looked at each other, debating whether to knock or climb back into their car and drive on.

Their decision was made for them, quite without warning, the front door swung open, and a giant Negro in the worn livery of a butler towered over them. His short-cropped kinky hair was snow-white—as were the irises of his eyes, which remained fixed on a point just above Tom's prickling scalp. Involuntarily, Jean gasped and edged closer to her husband, staring up at the man—who was almost seven feet tall. At her slight noise, the milky eyes followed her; and they realized that he was blind.

"We…we wondered if…? I mean, we saw your sign. And it was raining so hard…" Tom's hearty voice gave out.

For the round of his vibrant young baritone seemed to startle the giant Negro. His eyes, like white agates with their film of cataracts, widened. His lips trembled, then pressed together firmly, as with an effort of self-control.

"S-sometime I kin hear 'em…I kin hear 'em real plain!" he mumbled, obviously talking to himself. Then, with a sweeping bow reminiscent of a more gracious era when the old mansion was new, he stood aside and gestured them into the hall. "Come in, Suh! And…and Ma'm. Faraday House makes you welcome! Miss Addie seen you though a window o' de parlor, and say: 'Saul, you go open de door for our guests! Hit ain't a fit night for *ducks* to be out in!' Miss Addie say…"

Prattling on in a high childlike voice, the huge Negro ushered them through the door, bowing and scraping. With apprehensive lifts of the eyebrows, the newlyweds took off their wet coats and hung them on an ornate deerhorn hatrack. They followed uncertainly as the butler beckoned them toward a doorway down the long hall that was lighted only by candles in a series of shimmering crystal candelabra.

"Miss Addie right in here, in de parlor!" the tall Negro gestured again, with a bow. "Her and de…de other guests…"

Tom and Jean, walking very close together, trailed after him, and peered uncertainly through a door indicated by his sweeping black hand. At the threshold, they paused—aware first of a great paneled room; shabby now with its rotting brocades and velvet draperies, but still as beautiful and inviting as in the days when gray-uniformed soldiers and lovely women in crinoline must have laughed and chattered here.

A LOG fire burned in the fireplace, throwing distorted shadows over the room with its exquisite Colonial furniture and antique bric-a-brac. From a chair near the fire, as they entered, a little old lady rose with the quick fluttering motions of a bird, and came to meet them, smiling with a strange mixture of pleasure and regret on her wrinkled face. She wore a black-lace dress with a velvet collar, pinned at the neck by a handsome coral-and-pearl brooch that matched the coral earrings in her pierced ears. Silvery hair was piled up on her head in a quaint style, many years out of fashion, and fastened thus with a pearl-and-coral comb. By her gala attire, also by their sudden awareness of several other people in the room, Tom and Jean were taken aback.

"Oh..." Jean murmured. "I...we didn't mean to break in on a...a private party!" she apologized. "Perhaps you don't take tourists any more?"

"Tourists?" The old lady laughed gently at the word, as though she found it secretly amusing. "Oh! Oh, yes, my dear. You and your...your husband?" She glanced astutely from the ring on Jean's hand to Tom's uniform, then nodded. "You and your young soldier-husband are quite welcome here. Newly-weds?" She clucked her tongue at Jean's shy nod and Tom's flush. "How sad," she murmured. "But at least you're together. Sometimes those who stop here alone are so frightened, so bewildered...!"

Tom and Jean looked at her blankly. Then Tom grinned, interpreting her queer words in terms of his uniform and the current war.

"Oh! Yeah... And you say we can get a room for the night? Do you serve meals?"

"Anything you like." The old lady called Miss Addie nodded her head kindly. "Anything to make you...comfortable, until you're ready to...to go on. Would you like to register?" She gestured toward a dog-eared book on the table, beside which lay a quilled pen and an old-fashioned ink bottle quite empty of ink."

"Yes, of course!" Tom stepped briskly to the table, and flipped open the book. Riffling through the pages to find the last one bearing the present date, he frowned slowly...

The last page, which bore signatures and addresses of registrants, was yellow with age—and was dated ten years ago! He started to lift the pen, then laid it down again, puzzled.

If Miss Addie Faraday kept "overnight guests" for a living, Tom thought, she and her rundown tourist-home were not doing much business. Either that, or her guests—even those now moving restlessly around the friendly, firelit room—did not comply with the national law requiring all paying roomers to register. Something very odd was going on here.

"I...believe I'll register later," Tom said cautiously, glancing around at the other occupants of the room. "Will that be all right?"

"Quite all right," Miss Addie nodded amiably. "And now... Would you like to go straight to your room? I see you have no luggage..."

Tom dug into his pocket at once. "It's...it's still in the car. But we want to pay in advance, anyway..." He fumbled in another pocket, a slow flush creeping over his face. "Gosh! Can't seem to find my...my wallet...! Could I have dropped it when we...we got out of the car?"

Old Miss Faraday's expression of gracious welcome did not change, except for a slight quirk of kindly amusement at the corner of her wrinkled mouth. She held up her hand, speaking calmly, soothingly, as to an upset child.

"Don't trouble yourself about it. You can pay me when you...check out. And Saul will take care of your luggage...*Saul?*" She raised her sweet, birdlike voice, and the giant Negro reappeared in the doorway. "This gentleman thinks he may have dropped his wallet outside. Will you look for it, please? And their luggage? Of course, there's no hurry..."

There was, Tom noted with growing suspicion and annoyance, a definite note of amusement in the old lady's voice, as though she were playing some sort of game—a secret game in which the tall butler shared, somewhat sulkily.

"Yas'm," he bowed. "Anything else, Miss Addie?"

"No...no." His mistress fluttered a hand pleasantly. "Not just now. Perhaps later the young people will like a snack served in their room. Honeymoon-style...eh?" From somewhere in the folds of her lace gown, she actually produced a little ivory fan, and pretended to tap Tom's wrist with it playfully. "Partridge? Saul shot two or three yesterday, out in the north pasture. His dog, Feather, has been trained to bark when she points. Saul fires at the sound of their wings. Partridge—he's quite lucky with partridge. They *whir*, you know..."

"No kidding?" Tom, a demon-hunter himself, could not help a boyish exclamation at her words. "Say, honey, did you hear what...?"

HE TURNED to Jean—and broke off as their eyes met. The gracious air of hospitality about this old house, with its tiny silver-haired hostess and its giant black menial, was an insidious force disarming and relaxing him like the fire blazing on the hearth. His eyes traveled swiftly over the other occupants of the room—transients, evidently; a hodgepodge assortment of tourists who were acquainted neither with Miss Addie nor with one another.

His alert gaze singled out one—an elderly man wearing, of all things, a pair of stained overalls and a battered old strawhat. He was pacing about nervously, a distraught look on his weatherbeaten face, when Miss Addie moved to his side with the casual air of a good hostess drifting about among her guests.

"Can I get you something, sir?" she asked in that caroling voice like a songbird's. "Do sit down by the fire and rest yourself. You mustn't fret. Really, there's nothing to worry about...*now.*"

The old man, a farmer from his speech and dress, gave her a quick, seemingly desperate look, twisting his gnarled hands together.

"Ma'm—how'd I git here?" he blurted all at once, in a voice edged with hysteria. "I...I don't recollect *nothin'*! Except, I went out to put the cow in the barn, h'it was a-rainin' so hard. And then that sharp pain struck me, right here in the chest! I called to Sarah, that's m' sister, she's bedridden... And I kinda remember walking along some dark *road* or other... Then, all at once, I'm *here!*... Who...? Where...? I got to git back to Sarah! She can't *do* for herself! She's paralyzed...!"

"There, there." Miss Addie's quiet voice edged into his outburst, like a lark's singing in a lull of gunfire. "You mustn't be frightened or worried about your sister. Someone will take care of her. I'll phone the county health officer, if you'll tell me your name and address..."

"Wilkins. I got a little farm," the man blurted out eagerly. "Two mile east of Hopper's Ferry, on Highway 6. There's...there's just me and m' sister. But I got a boy in Atlanta! He'd come a-runnin' if he knew his aunt...if he knew I... *No!*" He shook his head stubbornly. "No, I got to git back someway! There's the stock, and there's my crop o' cotton..."

"Please." The mistress of Faraday House spoke again, melting his hysteria with gentleness. "You must get hold of yourself. *And...you must realize that you can't go back. You can only go...on, Mr. Wilkins.*"

Frankly eavesdropping, Tom and Jean stared at each other in blank astonishment. *Why* couldn't this frantic old farmer go back to his work and his bedridden sister? Why was Miss Addie telling him that in such a sad, gentle manner? Her soothing voice was insistent, almost hypnotic. Under its spell, a drowsy peace pervaded the room. Its occupants stopped shifting about. Voices lowered to a calmer pitch...

Jean started. Something like a chill breeze had brushed her bare arm. Looking down, she was aware of a thin, hollow-eyed little girl, about seven years old, staring up at her with an almost terrifying intensity. She was wearing...Jean gasped. Why, the child had on a pink flannel nightgown, and was barefooted! Perhaps she had wandered downstairs, she decided quickly, away from sleeping parents yet unaware that she had slipped out of bed.

The child's lips parted slowly in a vague, wistful smile.

"Are...are you my mother?" she whispered unexpectedly. "Daddy said I would...would see my Mommy soon! But I don't..." The thin mouth quivered. "I don't know what she *looks* like! She went away when I was borned, and...and there was only a snapshot Daddy had. Her hair was long and goldy, like yours!" she added, hopefully. "You *do* look kind of like the picture...!"

JEAN'S heart contracted. She reached out to gather the child into her embrace. *Poor little thing,* she thought fiercely. Deserted once by her mother, and now tossed back to her by a father who evidently did not want her either...! Her reaching hands almost touched the thin arms. But shyly, fearfully, the little girl backed away at her words:

"Darling—no. No, I'm not your Mommy... But aren't you cold, running around in your little nightgown and bare feet?" Jean smiled and held out a hand coaxingly. "Come let me take you back up to your room. Is your Daddy asleep upstairs? Does he know you've slipped out...?"

The child's dark eyes stared up at her. The pale lips puckered—with disappointment, or bewilderment, or something Jean could not define.

"I...don't know where my Daddy is, either!" she whimpered, near tears. "He was at the hospistle, right by my bed. And he...he was *crying!* And telling me about my Mommy, about how I'd be seeing her soon... You're *sure* you're not my...?" she asked again, with pathetic eagerness.

Tom and Jean exchanged a helpless look, torn with pity.

At that instant, Miss Addie drifted over to them, smiling kindly from the child to Jean in a way that puzzled the newlyweds.

"Look over there in that glass case!" the old lady said cheerily to the little girl. "It's just chockfull of china dollies I used to play with, when *I* was a little girl! That's the one. Yes!..." As the child, bemused, moved toward the cabinet across the room, the old Lady sighed. "Oh *dear!*" she murmured. "It's always like this with the children. Unless someone who's gone...on ahead comes back for them, to show them the way. Did she mention a mother?" Miss Addie asked hopefully.

"Why...why, yes!" Jean and Tom, over the silvery head, exchanged a shocked look. "A mother who deserted her as a baby! Who's supposed to meet her and... Look," Jean snapped. "You don't mean that poor little tike has nobody *with* her? She's traveling *alone?*"

"Most of them are." Miss Addie shrugged cryptically. "That's...that's why they stop here. Because they can't go back, of course—and they're afraid to go on. You're two of the *lucky* ones!" Her faded blue eyes traveled sadly from Tom to Jean. "You're together, so it isn't as...confusing. Oh *mercy!*" She broke off, fluttering her ivory fan in delicate agitation. "Can't you take the child on with you, if no one comes for her? The older ones do that, lots of times. Really, she'd be no trouble."

Jean gaped at her. *"Take...?* You're asking *us* to...?"

She broke off, startled, as wind or a sudden freshet of rain clattered a window of the firelit room. Glancing toward the sound, the honeymooners pointed and cried out at the sight of a dim face pressed against the panes—a woman's face, framed by long flowing hair the color of Jean's.

AT THEIR exclamation, the little girl, peeking forlornly at Miss Addie's doll-collection, turned. An expression of wonder and delight illuminated her thin features at sight of the face outside the window.

"Mommy! There's my Mommy...! I'd know her anywhere...!"

The words seemed torn from her, a glad cry, trailing after her as she pelted, barefoot, into the hall. The dim face vanished from the window, and Jean and Tom heard the front door open and close. But what amazed them most was the look of beaming complacence on the face of old Miss Faraday, fluttering her dainty fan with a new composure.

"Well," the old lady said in pleased voice, *"that's* settled. And now, if I can only make that poor Mr. Wilkins understand! Saul tells me I *simply can't* afford any more long-distance calls, or I'd just phone that son of his in Atlanta...hmm. There must be *some* way to help..."

Pursing her wrinkled lips, Miss Addie bustled across the room to another guest—a disheveled youth with a nasty looking bruise on his forehead. The honeymooners glanced at each other sharply as the old lady's clear, birdlike tones drifted to their ears:

"Young man...? Are you quite comfortable? Is there anything you'd like? Anyone I can...notify?"

The boy, a defiant look on his face, glared up at her from where he sat, hunched on a brocade loveseat. He reached into his sport jacket, mouth quivering, then searched another pocket, muttering under his breath.

"Nah!" he snarled. "How'd I get here? Tell me that! I know when my jalopy blew a tire...but after that, I...I... Who brought me here? What kind of a joint *is* this, anyhow? And how much is it gonna cost me? ...And where the hell is my pint?" His voice rose, savagely defensive, like that of a wild creature trapped in an animal-pit. "I had almost half a pint left in my...!"

Miss Addie sat down beside him serenely, not ruffled in the least by his youthful belligerence.

"Your whiskey?" she said pleasantly. "Perhaps you drank it, son, and...and threw the flask away, just before your...your accident... So *many* of them these days!" She clucked her tongue sadly. "I've had seven this month, would you believe it?

Young people, all of them. *So* young, like yourself—with so many good years ahead of you!"

The boy's face twitched. Bleary eyes peered at Miss Addie as through a fog, widening slowly as he seemed to understand more than her casual conversation offered on the surface.

"You…you mean I'm…?"

Tom and Jean heard his hoarse, frightened curse. "That quick, huh?" His defiant mouth twisted wryly, his fingers snapping with a small *pop* that might have been a twig breaking on the hearth. "Just like that, and it's all over?"

OLD MISS FARADAY smiled. "All over? My *dear!* It's only the *beginning!* 'To sleep; perchance to dream…' That was what bothered Hamlet, you know. Because, he wasn't *sure* it was the end. Just *pouf!* Just…oblivion. Which, of course, it *isn't!*" The ivory fan fluttered, almost flirtatiously, in front of the young man's face. "That's what these poor—well, the ones who do it themselves, believing it's a way out— That's what *they* discover, almost at once! There was one who came here last April, a young girl who had…ah, made rather a mess of her life and had decided she couldn't face the music. But, naturally," Miss Addie's cheery laugh rose above the subdued murmur of other voices in the quiet room, "she still had the same problems. Only, she couldn't *get at* them. She couldn't go back and work them out, poor and…and fix things. She sat around here, weeping and blaming herself, for weeks! Because there was a very simple solution to her problem, if she'd only sat down and thought it out, instead of… But then, of course," the old lady shrugged placidly, "it was too late. She couldn't go back and…and fix things. She had to go on, with her life ahead complicated by what she had left undone… Poor child! If she'd only used her…her body more constructively, while she had one."

The boy hunched beside her nodded miserably. "Yeah… That goes for me, too, huh?"

"That goes for everybody, at some time or another," Miss Addie said gently. "So, it's wicked to complicate...living for those we leave behind us to straighten out. You understand?"

The youth jerked his head in another helpless nod. "Sure, sure! *Now* you tell me—!" he burst out, bitterly sarcastic.

"Why, I'm pretty sure your parents told you the same thing," old Miss Faraday said, in a mildly chiding manner. "Or your pastor, or some favorite teacher. Or...well, if you had any gumption, you'd have just figured it out for yourself!"

The boy grinned sheepishly. "All right! So I knew better! What do I do now? How can I...?" His face crumpled again in sudden youthful dismay. "How can I ever make it up to Mom? And...and Dad? What can I *do...?*"

Old Miss Faraday gave a little shrug, oddly comforting in its finality, despite its gentle reproof.

"You'll have to leave it up to your brothers and sisters, if you have any," she said briskly. "Maybe *they* can make up for...the things you say you've done or left undone. As for now," she smiled at the boy, not unkindly, "you must go on. And try to do better at...the next place. You realize," she added sternly, "you won't be given the same chances as...as, say, that old Mr. Wilkins over there? Poor man, he's done his best. So I'm sure he'll be given wonderful advantages where he's going. If he can only reconcile himself to the fact that he *can't go back!*"

JEAN and Tom, still frankly listening in on these double-entendre conversations, nudged each other. Their puzzled eyes drifted to a little group of three oddly-assorted people near the fireplace: a crabbed old man, a leggy bobby-soxer chewing gum, and a wizened little man with slanted eyes who looked as if he might be a Chinese laundry-man. As they stared, Miss Addie drifted back to them, following their look with a faint smile.

"The 'flu epidemic," she explained lightly. "They've been comparing symptoms all evening! Ah, well—it gives them something in common," she laughed with a gay flutter of her fan. *"They* won't be lonely on the way, those three, for all they're so different!"

Tom cleared his throat nervously. "Uh...I wonder, could we go up to our room now? And have that little snack you promised? Partridge!" He smacked his lips, winking at Jean. "I don't suppose you'd have any wine? A dry wine, like Sauterne?"

"Why, yes," their tiny hostess bobbed her silver head graciously, "I believe there's a bottle or two left, down in the wine cellar. My brother was fond of good wine," she said pleasantly, "though he never drank too much for...safety, like that nice boy over there. Such a biddable lad!" Miss Addie glanced back at him, still hunched on the loveseat with his tousled head in his hands. "What a pity!"

"He...was in some kind of car accident?" Tom asked cautiously.

"Yes." The blue eyes flitted from him to Jean, with a sad look of understanding. "Like you two," and before they could correct her, she hurried on: "Saul will bring up your luggage presently...er...as soon as he can. Did you see a door just at the head of the staircase? That room will do nicely for you. Just go on up, won't you? I...I really must stay down here with these other poor dears. Some of them are...really quite troubled, as I'm sure you've noticed. I must do what I can to...to comfort them. May I look in on you later in the evening?" She beamed at them, almost fatuously. "It's such a pleasure to have guests who have...well, as Saul says, decided to cooperate with the inevitable!"

"Yes...sure! D-drop up to see us later..." Tom gulped.

SWAPPING another bewildered look the honeymooners left the parlor with its queer collection of occupants, and mounted the great curving staircase that swept upward from the hall. Pressed close to his side, Jean whispered:

"What's going *on* here? That weird old lady! Telling everybody they 'can't go back', that they must 'go on'! And that little girl...! Why, she ran out into the rain in her *nightgown,* Tom!

And Miss Faraday didn't even try to stop her! And that poor old farmer—*why* can't he go on back to his sister who's bed-ridden? Did you ever *hear* anything like that old woman...?"

"No, I never did!" Her husband laughed shortly. "You know what I think?" he growled. "I think that big Negro picked my pocket as I came in the door! And...and they're going to steal our luggage and maybe sell the car... Look, baby," he stopped grimly on the stairway, listening to the faint voices below, "we're getting out of here! We...why, I wouldn't spend the night in a creep-joint like this for all the tea in...*Oh-oh!*"

His words ended in a curse. At the head of the dim-lighted stairway the giant Negro, Saul, was looming like a dark genie waiting to show them into their room. There was a tray in his great ham-like hand—a tray set for two, with a delicious-looking grilled partridge for each of them, and a wicker-covered bottle of Sauterne. In spite of how his stomach knotted with apprehension, Tom's mouth watered. They had not eaten, he remembered, since breakfast—many hours and miles away from this strange old house just north of the Florida Line.

"Miss Addie say, 'Put dem young honeymooners in de Lavendar Room'!" The tall servant was prattling, again bowing and gesturing them through an open door. "And here de part-ridge and de wine y' all done ordered, suh. Compliments o' de house! ...*All dis-yeah good food,*" his childish voice sank to a mumble, "*goin to waste! Cook, cook, cook!*" Saul mumbled pettishly. "*Don' nobody but me and Miss Addie eat ary bite o' all dem victuals! Feather, he goin live high dis week! Us two cain't eat all dat stuff she tell me to fix for de guests...!*"

Hesitantly, rolling their eyes at each other, Tom and Jean entered the bedroom, not daring to antagonize that giant black. Blind he might be—but he could crush them between those two great hands, wring their necks like chickens before they could cry out. *If,* Tom thought helplessly, any of those bizarre people downstairs would come to their aid...!

"Th-thanks," he stammered, as Saul lit a beautiful hand-painted lamp beside the tester-bed and set his loaded tray alongside it.

"Er...I'd like to tip you, but I...I don't seem to have any change on me..." Tom fumbled in his pockets again, a reflex-action. "You didn't find my wallet outside in the drive did you? And what about our luggage?"

The agate-eyes of the blind Negro fixed on a point above his head, polite but sulky—as though Tom should have known better than to ask such a foolish question. As no doubt he should have, Tom thought grimly!

"Nawsuh. Ain't see no wallet, ain't had time to tote yo' luggage... *Wallet! Luggage!*" the childish voice fell to mumbling again, pettishly. *"Be mighty nice, now, if we did git holt o' some change-money! What wid de taxes pilin' up, an' us needin' a new well-pump, an'...Ma'm?"* The white eyes fixed on Jean as she whispered something urgently to Tom about getting out of there, possibly by the back door.

"N-nothing!" Jean quavered. "I...I was just saying what a pretty room this is!" she chattered nervously. "This lovely old four-poster bed..."

"Yas'm," Saul bobbed politely. "Dis-yeah Miss Addie's room. Ain't no others cleaned up... *And I ain't fixin' to do no dustin,' and makin' beds nobody don't sleep in!*" the huge Negro was mumbling again. *"Miss Addie say, "Have everthing like it was jest nachel. But I say, ain't no sense in it! Dem guests o' her'n ain't goin' eat nothing', ain't goin' sleep in no bed, and de biggest balance of 'em don't stay no time a-tall...! In and out, in and out...!"* The mumble continued irascibly, until at Tom's cough, Saul asked: "Anything else I can do for y' all, suh and ma'm? Miss Addie say, make you comf'able..."

"Oh, we're...very comfortable!" Tom managed, scanning the big high-ceilinged bedroom for another exit. There was only one, he saw with a sinking heart; and doubtless this ebon giant would station himself outside that door to make sure they did not escape.

"Den I'll bid you a good night, suh and ma'm!" Saul, with another old-world bow, backed through the door, but called back: "Miss Addie say she'll drap up to see y'all in a few minutes, after she 'tend to de other guests."

"Er...that's nice!" Jean said brightly, but as the door closed, her face took on an expression of dismay. "Oh, *Tom!*" she whimpered. "What are they planning? How can we get out of this...this...? That old lady is as crazy as a loon; you realize that, don't you?"

Her young husband nodded grimly. He tugged at his collar. "Yeah! That's pretty obvious! The thing I *don't* know is, what she has that big ogre of a servant *do* to her 'overnight guests!' Is this one of those murder-for-profit inns you read about...? Aw, honey!" his tone changed quickly as Jean's eyes dilated with terror. "I didn't mean to scare you. We'll get out of this...somehow!"

His pretty bride sank down on the tester-bed, removing her little flower hat and kicking off her shoes. The feather mattress sank under her invitingly, and she lay back, closing eyes dark-circled with fatigue.

"This is wonderful! I'm so-o tired... It seems we've been driving forever..."

Tom was eyeing the tray of partridge and wine. Tentatively he nibbled a piece, then shrugged and opened the wicker-covered bottle.

"If this is poisoned," he said airily, "it's a pleasant way to go! Mm-*mm!*" He smacked his lips over the delicate fowl. "Have some, honey?"

Jean grinned, and held out her hand for a browned wing. "What can we lose?" she pointed out wryly. "Oh, darling, I'm...I'm *scared!* What if...if they mean to...?"

She stopped speaking, with a gasp as a light knock sounded on the bedroom door.

"It's only I!" Miss Faraday's birdlike carol came through the closed portal. "May I come in?"

"Y-yes! Yes, come in...!" Jean called, sitting up with a panicky look at her husband.

They braced themselves as the door swung open, prepared for anything—even the sight of gigantic Saul following his mistress in with an axe in his great hands.

But Miss Addie was alone. She tiptoed in, still winnowing her small fan with coquettish grace, and sat down in a lovely old chair beside the bed. Tom and Jean watched her warily as she beamed up at them, sadness and humor an odd mixture in her expression.

"Well!" she said merrily. "I see you've made yourselves right at home. Saul will bring up your...er...luggage in a little while," she added in the placating voice of an adult promising a crying child the moon. "In the meanwhile, you just...rest. Hm? And...ah...accustom yourselves to...to...the realization that, although where you're going will be *different,* it won't necessarily be *worse* than...well, what you've just left behind!" she finished, like a diplomat carefully wording an important speech. "Are you beginning to understand? It's only that everyone fears change, and tries to cling to the familiar, the well-known..."

Tom did not dare look at his young wife. Elaborately casual, he strolled over to the bedside table again and took another delicious morsel from the tray. Somewhere he had heard that if one would humor a lunatic, and then carefully divert his attention from his obsession...

"Wonderful food...!" he murmured, and was opening his mouth for another bite when he noticed Miss Faraday staring at him. Her expression was that of supreme shock, bordering on consternation. She stood up, pointing a shaky finger at him.

"Why, you...you're *eating!*" she gasped. "And...and drinking!"

Tom lowered the morsel of bird and the tiny wineglass, stiffening. He looked at Jean, who was clutching her throat.

"Yes!" Tom snapped. "Of course I'm eating. Is the food poisoned?"

"No! No, certainly not!" Miss Addie panted, sinking back into her chair as if the shock of what she saw was too much. "It's only that...that...none of them ever...I mean, they only *think* they're hungry. It's just a thought-habit carried over from...from..."

She was interrupted by a loud hammering on the door. It burst open, and the blind Negro, drenched to the skin, plunged into the room. A damp wallet—Tom's wallet—was clutched in his outthrust black hand.

"Miss Addie!" he burst out in agitation, "Dey's a *car* out yonder in de driveway! I run slap into it a minute ago, when I went out to call Feather in out'n de rain! And...and he was totin' somep'm around in his fool mouth, like he always do—a slipper, or anything he pick up." Dark sensitive fingers ran over the object, seeing what the blind eyes could not. "Feel like a man's wallet! And hit's plumb full o' foldin'-money!"

"It's mine," Tom snapped, reaching out and taking it from the trembling black hand almost brusquely. "I *told* you I must have dropped it when we..."

"*Saul—!*" Miss Addie was fluttering her fan again, with a visible effort at composure. "Saul," she interrupted, half in dismay, half in amusement, "these two guests aren't like the others. They...I realized it when I saw this nice young man eating your partridge."

"*Eatin'!*" The white eyes bulged in the ebon face. "Y-you mean dey ain't...?"

"No," Miss Addie began to laugh weakly. "No, Saul, they're just like us," she turned to Jean and Tom then, with a gracious smile of apology. "You poor children! Stumbling out of the storm into a...a place like this! I naturally thought you were one of the usual...ah...travelers who stop here. We haven't had a genuine paying-guest," she confessed gaily, "for over ten years!"

THE tall Negro grinned feebly, nodding. "Naw'm. Sho' ain't." His face brightened as Tom shoved a damp bill into his hands. He felt it lovingly with a big callused thumb. *"Money!"* he said with a happy grunt. "Us sho' could *use* some! Them as ain't alive might not need it no mo', Miss Addie. But us two is *still livin'!"*

"From hand to mouth," Miss Addie said cheerfully. "Still..." She lifted her silver head proudly, "I haven't had to mortgage Faraday House. We manage. Of course, my hospital bills took all our savings—everything but the place and a few acres. Saul hunts and farms, even raises a little livestock. Now and then I sell off one of the family heirlooms when we're desperate for cash. ...But, there!" she broke off, engagingly. "I mustn't burden two lovebirds with my silly troubles! I only hope," she smiled apology once more, "that what you've seen here hasn't...upset you too much?"

Jean and Tom smiled back at her unsteadily. There was something so disarming about this sprightly old lady. And yet, obviously, she was a mental case! They stiffened once more at her next words; offered in a light conversational tone as if she were talking about the weather.

"You see, *they've* been coming here—the lost, bewildered ones like those you saw downstairs in the parlor—for eight years. Or is it nine?" she interrupted herself to peer up, bird-wise, at the giant Negro. "How long, Saul? Wasn't it 1945 when that policeman wandered in here, saying he had been shot in a holdup, in Traceyville? Poor thing! He kept trying to call headquarters, to give them a description of the bandit who shot him and wounded that gas-station attendant! As if it mattered to him *then!* Although," Miss Addie laughed, "we didn't realize...*what he was.* Not until after Saul took him upstairs. I called a doctor. But when we went up to the room, he was gone! There wasn't even any blood on the bedsheets and pillow, of course. Because...*they* have no substance. He only *thought* of himself as bleeding; so that's how I saw him, before he went on."

OVER her head, warily, Tom and Jean locked glances. *Crazy!* their eyes exchanged wordlessly. *But, harmless?* When would her lunacy take a dangerous turn...?

"Entirely weightless and without force of any kind," Miss Addie went on brightly. "That business about chain-rattling is ridiculous! They can't move solid objects, any more than a...a TV image could! Why, they can't possibly harm anyone or help one, either. That's what bothers them. One minute they can eat, drink, move heavy objects, fight, and so on. Then...*pouf!* They're no more than smoke. A thought-form, as I said. What we see is simply a...a *picture* of them, as they remember themselves. If they thought of themselves naked," the old lady tittered naughtily, "why, that's how we'd see them! But they think *clothes*, as well as *hair* and *skin* and so on. Even watches and jewelry, sometimes! Anything they feel strongly was a part of their personality in the...the material world they have just left. Of course, to *see* them, one must be either psychic...or very tired, ill, or feverish—any condition that would let the Sixth Sense come into play."

"Oh! I...I see," Jean gulped. "What you're trying to tell us," she stammered lamely, "is that...those people downstairs are...are all...?"

"Yes," old Miss Faraday inclined her head daintily. "Quite right, my dear. I don't know why they come *here!*" She laughed, with a merry flirt of the little fan. "Unless," she pursed her lips pensively, "it's because *I* died, and they feel a...a sort of kinship..."

Jean rolled her eyes at her husband. Tom, sipping his wine, choked.

"You...*d-died?*" he coughed. "Then you think you...uh...I mean, you're like them, too?"

"Oh, no!" Miss Addie emitted a silvery laugh full of innocent merriment. "No, no, I'm very much alive *now*. As alive as you are, you two nice young people! But I did die, about ten years ago—1943, wasn't it, Saul? Medically, you understand. There are degrees of death, as it is accepted by…ha, ha! What we call scientific fact." The fan brushed away Science airily, as if it were an annoying insect. "Some years ago, if breathing stopped, one was considered dead. But then they found a way to use artificial respiration, and make the lungs work again. Before that, consciousness was considered 'life'—and the unconscious were medically 'dead.' Many people in a state of trance were even buried alive, during the early days of medicine. But medicine is making such strides, there may come a day when the soul can be switched from one body to another! Naturally, a body is only a clumsy container for one's real *self…*"

Tom ran his finger around under his collar, moving across the room to Jean's side. They sat, very close together, under the canopy of the big bead where General Beauregarde, or Robert E. Lee, might very well have slept once. The old lady's matter-of-fact voice, reeling out mad words that, somehow, sounded so amazingly sane, held them spellbound with attention.

"Later in this century," Miss Faraday was saying, "a person was not pronounced 'dead' unless he had no pulse. Stimulants were used to start it up again; but if they failed, that was all. And that," she announced blandly, "was what happened to *me*. My heart stopped beating during an emergency operation to remove my appendix. Right there on that very bed you're sitting on! It was too late to rush me twenty-eight miles to the hospital in Mentonia. So…I died. My spirit left my body."

The newlyweds gaped at her. Miss Addie chuckled at their expressions.

"That is," she continued, her faded eyes twinkling, "I was dead for about thirty seconds. The doctor Saul phoned was out, and a young assistant came in his place. It was he who operated…and he had once happened to witness a miracle-operation by one of the big surgeons at Johns-Hopkins. A…a *tho…*" The old lady wrestled with her failing memory, then came up with the medical term: "A *thoroctomy*. You know?

176

Where the surgeon opens the chest cavity and massages the heart until it starts beating again? This young doctor of mine decided to try it on me. I was dead—so there was nothing to lose, he figured. And it worked!" Miss Addie bowed, fluttering her fan complacently. "I was brought back from the dead. Like Lazarus—poor man!" she added thoughtfully. "I know now why he was so *quiet,* afterward. There's so much I could tell you!" she sighed. "But I can't prove it, so nobody would believe me. Therefore, I've just learned to keep my mouth shut, and let them find out for themselves! Everyone will find out—sooner or later."

The newlyweds pressed closer together, disturbed yet soothed by an air of calm knowledge in their hostess's manner. Rain whispered against the windowpanes. Somewhere a dog howled mournfully, as though to emphasize the old lady's last sentence.

"Dat Feather!" Saul grunted suddenly, jolting them from their dream-like trance. "Hollerin' his haid off 'cause he wet and cold! I'm got to go down and fotch him into de kitchen..." Still mumbling, the blind giant lumbered out, groping his way with uncanny accuracy through the old house he had grown up in, and which was his whole world.

MISS ADDIE glanced after him fondly. She sighed. "My, I don't know how I'd get along without Saul! He's the grandson of a Faraday slave, and I'm willing this place to him when I die... When I *really* die!" she added, with a twinkle of humor in her eyes. "He does put up with a lot from me, Saul does. Especially about my...overnight guests! He can't see them, of course, and he *claims* he can't hear them! Whether it's only because they make so much extra work for him, I don't know," she smiled. "I...try to make them feel as natural as possible when they come here," she explained gently. "Poor things— they fight against going, some of them! Most are just bewildered. All they want is well, road-information. Or just a place to pause and think, until they get over the shock of suddenly being dead!"

"Oh! Oh, yes...I...I can see that," Jean managed a sickly smile. She squeezed Tom's hand, unseen by the old lady, signaling him as she said: "It's...been wonderful, stopping by here. And we want to pay for the full night. But...we really must go on, now that the storm has slacked up some. Er...what we wanted, too, was road-information. Are we far from Eltonville? I have an aunt there," she lied desperately. "We...er...we promised to stay overnight with her, and if we don't do it, this near...I'm sure you understand?"

Old Miss Faraday's blue eyes searched Jean's face knowingly. She smiled, with a tiny, almost invisible shrug.

"Of course, dear," she said graciously. "Of course I understand. Eltonville is only eight miles on from here. A nice hotel there. Really, a haunted house," her eyes twinkled, "is no place for a honeymoon. Eh?"

"Oh, I...I didn't mean...!" Jean floundered. "It's only that..."

"Yes!" Tom came to her rescue. "This aunt of my wife's— she's expecting us. And if we don't come rolling in sometime tonight...she's liable to think...uh..."

"...that you've joined my...my 'overnight guests?'" the old lady finished, with a sly wink. "You may have noticed my sign as you drove in," she added, with girlish giggle of mirth. "Did you look at it closely? You know, I sometimes wonder if *it* isn't the reason they use Faraday House as a...a sort of way station, I call it. I wonder if there are other way stations, like this one? Places where they...? If I were sure it *wasn't* what brings them here, I'd take it down—that sign," she smiled. "We really don't take overnight guests any more. At least, not the kind who expect A-1 accommodations! I'm too old...and it makes too much work for Saul, cleaning and carrying luggage and the like. Besides," Miss Addie said complacently, "I manage to get along without money, in this little halfway house of mine! Halfway between life and death, one might say... Oh! You leaving now? I'll see you to the door..."

STEERING down the winding gravel drive a few moments later, Tom and Jean looked back through the rain at the big white-columned house. They had left, they realized, in rather an abrupt hurry—without even a glance into that peaceful, firelit parlor, where had been assembled such an unusual assortment of people. Bidding Miss Addie good-bye hastily, they had dashed out to the little car standing in the rain—almost tripping over a friendly-looking Irish setter, which trotted back into the house at a whistle from the butler. The great front door had not even closed before Tom started the motor and took off in second-gear.

But now, at the end of the driveway, Tom braked the car, strangely loathe to lose sight of that hospitable old mansion, with its quaint bird-like hostess and childlike black genie of a servant. They turned, looking back for a long thoughtful moment. Then Tom laughed shortly, patting his young bride on the knee.

"Of course you know," he chuckled, "those...*guests* weren't there at all. We've been victims of mass-hypnosis. What with that old lady's insane playacting, and our own exhaustion...why, we were a push-over!"

Jean laughed shakily, snuggling against him. "Hypnosis?" she echoed obediently. "She believed so firmly, she made us believe? Naturally—" Her tone became brisk and matter-of-fact, if still a bit quavery—"there is no such thing as a...a..." She broke off abruptly, pointing up at Miss Addie's gatepost, now more visible since the rain had slacked to a drizzle. *"Tom!"* she whispered. *"That sign of her's...* Look at it! *That's* what she was talking about: that maybe *it* was what drew them here! ...See what the wind and rain have done to those letters, the *u* and the *e* in *Guests...?"*

Her husband craned to see...and gave a yelp of mirth. Jean giggled. They were still laughing-gaily, intimately, somehow no longer afraid of being parted by a grim shadow called *Death*—as they drove on down the highway through the rainswept night.

For, what the sign on the gatepost, on closer inspection, had seemed rakishly to advertise was:

FARADAY HOUSE
Miss Adelaide Faraday, Prop.
Overnight Ghosts

THE END

VICTIM OF THE YEAR

By Robert F. Young

There were several women in his life…and one of them was a witch who had selected him to be the…

HAROLD KNOWLES had been seeing the small brunette every Monday morning for the past six months, but their trysts were of an official rather than a romantic nature, and up until the Monday morning when he signed for his final unemployment-insurance check he had considered her no more noteworthy than the other are-you-ready-willing-and-able-to-work-sign-here-please girls who shared her duties with her behind the claimants' counter. True, he had wondered once or twice why she would never meet his gaze and on several occasions he had been mildly, if perversely, tempted to reach across the counter and tweak the wispy bangs that curled along her forehead; but up until the moment when she slipped the note into his claimant's folder that was about as far as either his curiosity or his interest had taken him.

Immediately after performing the aforementioned act, she handed him the folder and leaned over the counter. For the first time her eyes met his, and he was astonished at their blue naïveté. Read this as soon as you get home," she whispered. "It's important!"

Several buildings from the one that housed the employment office he stepped into a deserted store-entrance and withdrew the folder from his pocket. Pulling out the note, he unfolded it. For some time he stared uncomprehendingly at the two frost-kissed maple leaves it enclosed, then he transferred his attention to the message itself. It was written in a large, almost child-like, scrawl, but the character of its penmanship was by far its least remarkable quality.

Dear Harold (he read): *Tonight is Halloween and soon you will be in grave danger. I am a witch and I know about such things. As proof of my powers I am enclosing two magic leaves which will when you need them turn into $20 bills. As additional proof, I will make a prophecy. Your interview at Ackman Innovators, Inc. this afternoon will turn out the same way all your other interviews have turned out ever since you lost your job eight months ago: you will not get to first base. Meet me at five o'clock when I get through work and I will explain everything.*

GLORIA MAPLES

HE read the message again, momentarily expecting the words to realign themselves into sentences that made sense. They did nothing of the sort. Girls had written him silly notes before, but this one topped them all.

He shook his head in an attempt to clear his thoughts. Granted, tonight was Halloween, and granted, Halloween was supposedly the time of year when witches crept out of their cob-webbed closets and did barrel-rolls on brooms, and granted, his run of bad luck had reached a point where he half-believed that it was attributable to other than natural causes. But still and all—!

Gradually the world reassumed its sane and sensible aspect. The are-you-ready-willing-and-able-to-work-sign-here-please girl was putting on a witch-act in a naive attempt to attract his attention—that was all. Certainly, working as she did, less than an arm's length away from the job-placement section, she could have found out about his forthcoming interview with Mr. Ackman easily enough. And as for her magic leaves—

He laughed and started to throw them away. But for some reason he changed his mind and slipped them into his pocket in-stead. He wadded up the note and tossed it into a nearby refuse can; then, putting the incident from his mind, he returned to his rooming-house to get ready for his luncheon-date with his girl friend, Priscilla Sturgis.

There were several women in his life . . . and one of them was a witch who had selected him to be the . . .

Victim of the Year

By ROBERT F. YOUNG

Illustrator
SUMMERS

Old Mother Hubbard was in her kitchen, rattling pots and pans, when he tiptoed into the downstairs hall—he had taken to tiptoeing lately because of the twenty-dollars back-rent he owed her—and as she never closed her door except at night or when she went out, he glimpsed her as he passed it. She was standing tall and almost scarecrow-thin in front of the kitchen stove, still stubbornly wearing black in deference to the husband who had been dead now for nearly ten years. Her real name was Mrs. Pasquale, and she kept a cat instead of a dog; but one of her first roomers, inspired no doubt by the hunger that sometimes shone in her dark and liquid eyes, had started the sobriquet rolling, and she had been known as "Old Mother Hubbard" ever since.

His room still smelled of the canned chicken-soup he had heated for breakfast that morning, and he opened the window to air the place out. After shaving in the second-floor bathroom he combed his hair in his dresser mirror, then returned to the street. There, he lit the first of the three cigarettes he allowed himself each day and blew smoke into the October wind. On the stoop next door a little boy was industriously carving a grotesque mouth in a big pumpkin.

THE site for the luncheon date was a swank restaurant across the street from the department store where Priscilla held down the job of buyer. She was already there when Harold arrived, and he joined her at her table, afflicted with that curious combination of admiration, adoration and awe which the sight of her invariably evoked in him. She was sunlight and laughter made woman. Her eyes were as golden as October days and her hair was the hue of Indian maize; her smile was Indian summer. Small wonder that, in a vain attempt to augment his savings and thereby expedite their wedding date, he had exchanged his suburban apartment in Forestview for a cheap room in the city; small wonder that his bitterness over the misfortunes that had dogged his footsteps ever since should be all the more acute.

But you'd never have known from the warmth of her smile that in the space of eight months he had been reduced from a prosperous suburbanite to a near-penniless city-dweller with nothing between him and starvation but a five-dollar bill and a final unemployment-insurance check. "Hi, doll," she said. "Coming to my party tonight?"

"I—I don't know," he said, thinking of the outdated cut of his best suit and wondering, as he had the first time she'd asked him, why she hadn't made it a masquerade party in honor of the occasion.

"Oh, but you've just got to come, Harold! We're going to bob for apples and pin the tail on the donkey and dance and everything. Not only that, Uncle Vic is going to be there, and he's just dying to meet you!"

She was originally from out of town, and Uncle Vic, so far as Harold had ever been able to ascertain, was her only living relative. "All right," he agreed reluctantly. "What time does it begin?"

"Seven-thirty—and don't you dare show up a second later. Wait'll you see the Halloween cake I baked—it's out of this world!"

She only had an hour for lunch, and it flew by. Over their second coffees she told him about the palatial new elementary school with the two swimming pools which the Forestview citizens had voted to build and about how the school tax would double itself within five years as a consequence. He was not surprised: as a one-time denizen of the community he knew full well how the citizens doted on their offspring. Almost before he knew it, it was time to pay the check, and after signaling the waitress he reached into his pocket and pulled out what he thought was the lonely five-dollar bill. It was so crisp and new that it crackled between his fingers, and that was odd because when he had put it into his pocket it had been old and crinkled. Looking at it, he discovered that it had changed in other ways too: it had Andrew Jackson's picture on it instead of Abraham Lincoln's, and in each of its corners the numeral "20" stood out bold and clear.

An icy wind blew down the back of his neck and set his nerve-ends to tingling. Hurriedly he pulled out the pocket's remaining contents. They consisted of two articles: another crisp twenty, and the missing five.

He became aware that he was the focal point of two pairs of eyes. One pair—Priscilla's—were a lambent gold. The other pair—the waitress's—were an impatient hazel. Hastily he paid the check with one of the twenties, and after receiving his change, escorted Priscilla across the street to the department store. She looked at him curiously when they reached the entrance and he thought for a moment that she was going to question him about his sudden wealth. But she didn't. All she said was, "See you tonight, doll—'by."

HIS interview was scheduled for three o'clock. He killed the lion's share of the intervening two hours on a bench in the park, examining the pros and cons of the reality of witches. He arrived at the following conclusions: (1) in common with alchemy, witchcraft was a product of the dark ages and held up not one whit better in the uncompromising light of modern science; (2) there was a logical explanation behind the seemingly miraculous metamorphosis of the maple leaves (he didn't know what it was but he was darned if he was going to lose faith in the scientific light because of a dark corner or two); and (3) the are-you-ready-willing-and-able-to-work-sign-here-please girl knew about as much about sorcery as she probably knew about sex.

Feeling better, he left the park and took a bus to Ackman Innovators, Inc. The girl behind the receptionist's desk looked at him with hostile brown eyes when he handed her the card which he had received in the morning's mail from the job-placement division. She glanced at it, then promptly handed it back. "Mr. Ackman isn't in right now," she said coldly. "However, if he'd had an appointment to interview you I'm sure he would have told me."

Harold was dumbfounded. "But—"

"And anyway," the girl continued, "we're not doing any hiring at the moment. Come back in about two months."

"*Two months!* But this card says—"

"Two months," the girl repeated firmly. "Good day, sir."

It was a grim young man who stepped into the street a moment later and headed for the bus stop, and it was a grim young man who got off the bus some ten minutes later and made a beeline for the employment-office. The girl on duty behind the job-placement counter proved to be as much in the dark as he was. "Why don't you go back tomorrow?" she suggested. "In the meantime I'll—"

"Not in a million years!" he said. Turning to leave, he saw the are-you-ready-willing-and-able-to-work-sign-here-please girl who had slipped the note into his folder regarding him earnestly from behind the claimants' counter, and for the second time that day an icy wind blew down the back of his neck. He remembered her name: Gloria Maples. *Gloria, Maples,* he said to himself grimly, descending the stairs to the street. *Avocation-Witch.*

His new wealth rendered further adherence to his poverty-induced cigarette schedule unnecessary, so he bought a pack of filter-tips in a nearby drugstore; then he returned to the employment-office building and waited by the doorway till five o'clock came. He was halfway through his fourth cigarette when she finally stepped into the street.

Her blue eyes brightened when she saw him. "Hi," she said. "We'll go to my apartment—I can talk better there."

SHE lived in a third-floor walk-up in a rooming house almost as run-down as Old Mother Hubbard's. He followed her through a small kitchen into a slightly larger living room. It contained a battered mohair sofa, a battered mohair chair and a wobbly glass-topped coffee table. There was a three-legged black cat, with part of its tail missing, sleeping on the sofa.

Gloria sat down beside it, picked it up and placed it gently on her lap. "Matilda, this is Harold," she said. "Harold, this is my cat, Matilda."

Harold took the mohair chair.

"What happened to her other leg?"

"She got run over by a hit-and-run driver and I found her lying in the street and took her to a vet. He—he wanted to put her away but I wouldn't let him. Nobody ever claimed her so I kept her. A—a witch is supposed to have a black cat."

He looked at her contemplatively. Half an hour ago he had firmly believed her to be a witch; now the mere idea of such a thing seemed utterly preposterous. Why, she was as naive as a May morning! Naive or not, however, she still had some explaining to do. He fixed her with uncompromising eyes. "Please to begin," he said.

"I—I will." She stroked Matilda's back with nervous fingertips. "I'll—I'll begin at the beginning. First of all, I'm not a full-fledged witch yet—I'm an apprentice witch. You see, the coven-sisters in the various districts are always on the lookout for potential witches, and whenever they hear of someone who's discontented and bitter they contact her through their underlings and offer to send her through witch-school. It's only a one-year course, but they're awfully strict, and if you're caught doing something a respectable witch wouldn't do, you're disqualified. For—for instance, if the coven-sister who nominated you our class guinea-pig ever finds out I'm trying to help you she'll have me expelled immediately—and—and not only that, she may try to do me in too."

Harold lit a cigarette. He took a deep drag. "What?" he asked a little desperately, "is a class guinea-pig?"

"I—I was coming to that," Gloria said. "You see, each Candlemas the senior coven-sister of the three local covens nominates a Victim of the Year and turns him over to the apprentice-witch class till Allhallows Eve for them to practice their sorcery on. Then, on Allhallows Eve, she takes over and tries to do him in in some diabolical way. This—this year you were nominated.

MY—my classmates and I vied with each other in doing mean things to you. First we fixed it so you'd get laid off, and then we caused your ex-employer to tell the employment-office that you quit so you'd have to wait six weeks for your first unemployment-insurance check and wouldn't have enough money to keep up your payments on your car and would lose it, and ever since then we've been conjuring up antagonism toward you in the minds of the other local employers and their office personnel, and—and all the while I kept seeing you come in every week to sign for your checks and saw how frayed your sleeves were getting and—and how sad you were and—and—

Do—do you remember that quart of milk you brought home one time and it turned out to be sour when—when you got around to drink it? Well, I'm the one that soured it, and oh, Harold, I'm so ashamed of myself I could just lie right down and die!" And before his startled eyes she burst into tears and ran out into the kitchen.

Matilda had alighted on all three feet, and now she came over and began rubbing her furry sides against his pant-leg. He patted her head abstractedly, shaken in spite of himself. He *had* been laid off; his ex-employer *had* told the employment-office he had quit; he *had* lost his car—everything that Gloria had said, in short, was true.

Granted; but that didn't mean she was *responsible* for his job difficulties—it merely meant that she knew about them. And as an are-you-ready-willing-and-able-to-work-sign-here-please girl, how could she help knowing about them? As for the sour-milk incident, she could have gotten the information from Old Mother Hubbard; after all, it was the old lady's refrigerator that the milk had gone sour in.

Presently he heard her moving about in the kitchen, and in a little while she appeared in the doorway. "Come—come out and sit down, Harold," she said. "I—I fixed us some sandwiches."

THE sandwiches were peanut butter. He ate three and washed them down with two glasses of milk. She ate half a one and drank half a glass of milk. Some of the milk clung to her upper lip in a moist white film. "You've no idea how much better I feel, now that I've got my wickedness off my chest," she said. "You will be careful tonight, won't you? The best thing to do is stay where there's lots of people. It's hard for a witch to hex you when you're in a crowd."

He looked at her milk-mustache, growing more amused by the second. "I'm going to my girl friend's Halloween party, so I should be safe enough," he said.

She dropped her eyes. "I—I guess you'll be safe enough there all right. It would be better, though, if you stayed somewhere where there are plenty of policemen. Witches are leery of the law. Devil's deputies, too. His—his majesty insists on outward conformity and good citizenship, and if any of his employees get caught doing something even a little bit illegal, he gives them the ax, and bingo!—their power is gone."

"You mean 'the pitchfork', not the ax, don't you?" Harold said, holding back his laughter.

"This is no time to be facetious, Harold. Don't you realize that your very life is at stake?"

She got up and returned the bottle of milk to the refrigerator. Then she picked up the jar of peanut butter and carried it over to a tall cupboard by the sink. He gasped when she opened the door. Every one of the shelves was filled with similar jars, and in some cases they were piled two high.

"Good lord!" he said. "Is that all you ever eat?"

She faced him shyly. "Not—not exactly. I eat lunch in the cafeteria across the street from the office. I—I was never very good at cooking. Back home, mom did it all, and when I got transferred here there was no one to teach me."

He stood up. How she had prophesied the outcome of his interview he would probably never know, but one thing he did know: she wasn't any more to blame for the way it had turned out than she was to blame for the way all the others had turned out. After she got over her complex he would return the two twenties to her, and perhaps then she would explain how she had tricked him into believing when he had first looked at them that they were maple leaves. It would be futile to ask her now.

"Well, thank you for the sandwiches," he said.

She accompanied him to the door. Something about her forlorn aspect prompted him to give her Priscilla's telephone number. "In case you need me for anything," he explained. "And now I've got to go."

"Good—good by, Harold. And be very careful, please."

THERE were witches galore in the streets, not to mention goblins, ghosts, brownies and spacemen; however, he was in no mood for trick-or-treaters, and he hailed the first cab that came along. For some reason he couldn't get Gloria out of his mind. He was so pre-occupied with her, in fact, that when he entered the rooming-house he didn't remember to tiptoe till he came opposite Old Mother Hubbard's door and saw the old lady standing before the stove, stirring the steaming contents of a large black kettle with a long wooden spoon. It was too late then, for she had already heard him. Setting the spoon aside, she came swiftly through the doorway, hunger shining in her eyes, her black cat tagging at her heels.

He remembered the second twenty just in time and thrust it into her hand when she came up to him; then he brushed past her and hurried up the stairs. In his room he donned his best suit and surveyed himself in the dresser mirror. He could get by all right, he decided—provided that he stayed in the background. The background was where he belonged anyway.

Forestview was a half-hour's ride by bus, so the sooner he got started, the better. He descended the stairs, tying his tie on the way down. Old Mother Hubbard was nowhere to be seen, but the contents of her kettle were bubbling audibly and giving off a gamy odor that permeated the entire downstairs hall. He was glad when he reached the street. The sky was overcast and the air had grown appreciably cooler. Turning up his suitcoat collar, he headed for the bus stop. Thirty-five minutes later he arrived in Forestview.

Priscilla's house was a modern American-colonial and stood at the end of a maple-bordered street. Cars jammed its driveway and were parked along the curb halfway to the corner. Many of them had out-of-state license plates; in her capacity as buyer, Priscilla traveled a lot and met many out-of-town people. She answered his ring, resplendent in a sequined sheath. "Hi, doll, come on in," she said warmly. "Everybody's just dying to meet you!"

There were almost forty people present, and Priscilla must have praised him to the skies, judging from the enthusiastic way they responded when she introduced him. Especially Uncle Vic, who turned out to be a tall wiry individual in his sixties, with crew-cut white hair, keen blue eyes and a firm handclasp. "Come on out to the bar," he told Harold, "and I'll mix you a drink."

The "bar" was the breakfast counter. Uncle Vic made him a stiff highball. "Priscilla's quite a girl, don't you think?" he asked, handing it to him. "Wait'll you see some of the innovations she's dreamed up for a little later on in the evening!"

"Are you from around here, sir?" Harold asked, still somewhat dazed from Priscilla's resplendence.

"Oh yes. I'm district manager for Schierke and Elend Enterprises. Quite a famous international concern—though probably you've never heard of it. Let's join the others, shall we?"

PRISCILLA'S stereo was going full-blast and the living-room rug had been rolled up and stashed away in a corner. Priscilla was dancing with a tall young man as darkly handsome as she was radiantly beautiful. Harold, his diffidence routed by the highball he had drunk, cut in. She was feather-light in his arms, and her eyes were golden mirrors in which he saw the world, and the world was a roseate and wondrous thing.

Uncle Vic whirled by, a dark-haired dowager in his arms. He winked at Harold broadly. The lights grew soft, warm. Time tiptoed from the room—

Suddenly the ringing of the phone stabbed through the stereo-throb of the music. "Excuse me," Priscilla said, slipping from his arms and going into the hall. She appeared a moment later in the doorway, the receiver in her hand. "It's for you," she said.

He took the receiver from her and raised it to his ear. "Hello?"

"Harold?" It was Gloria's voice. "Are you all right, Harold?"

He was annoyed. "Of course I'm all right," he said gruffly. "Why shouldn't I be?"

"Be—because they found out about us—the coven-sisters, I mean. Tonight when I went to witch-class the head instructress told me I was through and that I'd get my come-uppance before midnight."

"Nonsense, Gloria! You've let this obsession of yours get the best of you."

"But it's not an obsession, it's real. Oh, Harold, I'm so scared!"

She was almost hysterical. Slowly his annoyance gave way before a mental picture of her sitting forlornly in her little living room, her blue eyes dark with terror. "All right," he said abruptly, "I'll come over for a while. Pull yourself together."

He hung up. Priscilla was standing in the living-room door-way looking at him oddly. "You'll have to excuse me for an hour or so," he said. "Something's come up."

"But doll, I was just going to start the games. At least stay long enough to help us pin the tail on the—the donkey."

"I'm sorry, Pris—I can't."

She came very close to him and playfully gripped his lapels. "I won't let you go unless you promise to come back."

"All right," he said. "I promise."

HE took a cab, hoping to save time, but a traffic jam thwarted him and it was a full forty minutes later when he climbed the three flights of stairs to Gloria's walk-up. When she failed to answer his knock he pushed the door open and stepped inside. He found her in the little living room, huddled on the mohair sofa, her shoulders shaking. On the floor at her feet lay her black cat, its three legs jutting grotesquely from its lifeless body.

He went over and sat down beside her and put his arms around her. Slowly her shoulders quieted. "She—she dropped dead about ten minutes ago," she said. "Oh why did they have to pick on her—*why?*"

Tears ran down her cheeks, and she pressed her face against his lapel. He saw the way it was with her now; now he understood. Young men like himself, laughing at her, treating her like a child when she wanted to be treated like a woman; buying her candy when she craved flowers. No wonder she had wanted to become a witch—and, conversely, no wonder she hadn't been able to become one. "How did they find out about us, Gloria?" he asked gently.

"The coven-sister who nominated you Victim of the Year learned that you had magic money in your possession—a witch can spot it right away—and told the head instructress. The head instructress was furious. She—she lined all of us up along the wall and threatened to torture us till one of us confessed, and I didn't want to see the other girls suffer so I said I was the one. What made it worse was that I've been sneaking into the coven library when no one was there and reading forbidden books. That's how I was able to energize the chlorophyll and induce the chromatolysis-effect that—"

His voice was cold. "Who is this coven-sister, Gloria?"

"I—I don't know. I've never seen any of them. An apprentice witch isn't permitted in their presence. But she must be someone you're acquainted with."

He stood up. "Never mind. *I* know who she is. I have to go now, Gloria, but I promise I'll be back."

OLD Mother Hubbard's door was closed. He pounded on it peremptorily. He pounded on it again. He tried the knob. It would not turn.

The gamy odor still permeated the hall. Probably, he thought bitterly, she had taken her unholy brew to the local Sabbat and was even now presiding over it with her gaunt unlovely sisters, the devil's deputy, in his woolly goat-robe, standing at her side. Well he would wait for her to return. He would sit on the stairs and wait till she came in the door and then he would tell her straight to her face what he thought of black-hearted old women who preyed on harmless girls and murdered crippled cats.

He got out his cigarettes, felt in his pocket for his matches. The folder was empty. There was another one in his dresser-drawer, he remembered, and he went upstairs to get it. Opening the drawer, he paused. On top of the dresser lay a crisp twenty-dollar bill. Beside it lay a sheet of yellow tablet-paper.

Wonderingly he picked the paper up. On it, the following words had been laboriously printed with a soft-lead pencil:

Every day when I clean your room I smell the canned soup you cook each night and morning and it is heavy on my heart that one so fine should suffer. Tonight I want to say, Harold, will you share with me the spaghetti with venison meatballs that I cook all afternoon on my stove, but you will not listen and you give me money and walk away. Now I give it back. Twenty dollars I will never need so much that good food someone cannot buy. I go now to St. Anthony's to say a prayer for you.

He stood there immobile for a long time, staring at the simple words. Hunger in a person's eyes did not always imply greed; sometimes it implied a need for understanding, a need to help; a need not to be alone.

At length he left the room and descended the stairs. The hall phone rang just as he was passing it. He took down the receiver. "Hello?"

"Hello," a man's voice answered. "I'd like to speak to Mr. Knowles."

"This is Mr. Knowles."

"This is Mr. Ackman. I hope you'll forgive me for having forgotten about our appointment this afternoon. Why I did, I don't know. Anyway, I just remembered it a moment ago—out of a clear blue sky, so to speak—so if you're still interested I'd like you to drop around tomorrow morning. I'm sure I can work something out for you."

"I'll say I'm still interested!" Harold said. "And thank you for calling."

HE took a cab back to Forestview. Halfway there, the plan came to him, and he had the driver stop at an all-night drugstore. After buying a cake of soap, he climbed back into the cab. During the remainder of the ride he occupied himself by figuring out the details. It was a simple plan, and there weren't very many of them; but thinking of them kept his mind off the sickness in the pit of his stomach.

After the driver let him off in front of Priscilla's he waited till the cab disappeared around the corner, then he soaped all the windshields of the cars standing in the driveway and along the curb, and removed the valves from all the tires. When he was finished he walked half a block to an all-night service station and made a phone call. Then he returned to Priscilla's.

The party was in full swing. Her eyes lit up when he walked in the door, and a few minutes later she brought in a cake from the kitchen and set it on a card table in the middle of the living room. It was a big three-layer cake with orange frosting. In its center stood two tiny wax dolls, and around them, arranged in the shape of a pentagram, were thirty-one candles. A glimmering of the truth struck him then, and he peered at the dolls intently. One of them bore a faint resemblance to him; the other bore a faint resemblance to Gloria.

Still he found it hard to believe. Not Priscilla of the golden eyes, the golden hair; not Priscilla of the golden soul. He saw the big rectangular poster hanging on the wall then, and he had to believe. It was the pin-the-tail-on-the-donkey poster, and there were scores of tiny pinpricks in the painted animal's body. Only the animal wasn't a donkey, it was a cat—a three-legged black cat with half a tail. It had a whole tail now, though—

Not that it would need one any more.

Priscilla was lighting the candles, and everyone was standing around the card table, looking at him eagerly. Greedily. He noticed something then—something that his previous absorption with Priscilla had wiped from his awareness. The women outnumbered the men by a ratio of twelve to one.

The candle flames leaped up in little flickering's and presently, as the wax dolls began to melt, he felt the first faint prickling of the heat. Uncle Vic leaned toward him, his face thinner somehow, his nose more pointed. Priscilla, her task completed, leaned toward him also. Her face was thinner too and her golden eyes had transmuted to a baleful yellow. Her lips were drawn back, revealing preternaturally pointed eyeteeth. It was a masquerade party after all, and the time for unmasking had come. He shuddered at the realization.

"But why, Priscilla?" he asked, fighting to control his horror. *"Why?"*

The yellow eyes incandesced. "You love me don't you? Well I'm returning your love in the only way I can. I'm returning it with hate—and I'm returning it in full-measure!"

HE drew back. The candle flames grew brighter, warmer. The first drops of sweat dampened his forehead. He held himself tight, listening with all his being. At last he heard the sound he was waiting for—the slamming of a car door. He relaxed then.

"What was that?" Uncle Vic asked sharply.

"The police, I imagine," Harold said. "I asked them to drop by."

"It can't be," Priscilla said shrilly. "Why, if you even mentioned the word 'Sabbat' they'd laugh at you!"

"I kind of thought they would—that's why I didn't mention it. I asked them to drop by for quite another reason. Wait'll you see what the kids have done to your cars."

She was staring at him. So was Uncle Vic. So were the others. "Our cars—" she began. Then, "Oh, you mean they soaped the windows and things like that." She laughed. "We'll simply refuse to prefer charges won't we, Uncle Vic?"

Uncle Vic relaxed visibly. "Sure, that's what we'll do."

"Who," Harold said, wiping his forehead, "said anything about you preferring charges?" He confronted Priscilla. "Obviously you aren't familiar with Forestview's ordinances.

197

The one I have in mind states that on the night of October thirty-first all private vehicles shall be kept in garages, either public or private, in order that our citizens of tomorrow will not be tempted to perform acts of a delinquent nature. The local kids have been behaving so well for the past several years that the ordinance has been unofficially laid to rest, but I imagine that once the chief of police hears about your flagrant violation of it he'll be delighted to revive it."

Abruptly Uncle Vic blew out the candles. "You fool!" he said to Priscilla. "You utter fool!" His voice rose. "The old man will be furious. He'll strip us of our powers—everyone of us. I'll lose my vicariate! Why didn't you check on the ordinances? Why didn't—"

"Shut up, you old goat!" Priscilla screamed. "He's lying, don't you see? The police aren't there! There's no one out there! He's lying, I tell you. He's—"

The doorbell rang.

It was nearing midnight when Harold got back to the city. But late though the hour was, there was still time to go trick-or-treating. First he would pick up Gloria, he decided, and then the two of them would go calling on Mrs. Pasquale. And if the old lady didn't come across with two plates of her spaghetti with venison meatballs they would soap her windows but good.

THE END

If you've enjoyed this book, you will not want to miss these terrific titles…

ARMCHAIR SCI-FI & HORROR DOUBLE NOVELS, $12.95 each

D-11   **PERIL OF THE STARMEN** by Kris Neville
       THE FORGOTTEN PLANET by Murray Leinster

D-12   **THE STAR LORD** by Boyd Ellanby
       CAPTIVES OF THE FLAME by Samuel R. Delaney

D-13   **MEN OF THE MORNING STAR** by Edmund Hamilton
       PLANET FOR PLUNDER by Hal Clement and Sam Merwin, Jr.

D-14   **ICE CITY OF THE GORGON** by Chester S. Geier and Richard Shaver
       WHEN THE WORLD TOTTERED by Lester Del Rey

D-15   **WORLDS WITHOUT END** by Clifford D. Simak
       THE LAVENDER VINE OF DEATH by Don Wilcox

D-16   **SHADOW ON THE MOON** by Joe Gibson
       ARMAGEDDON EARTH by Geoff St. Reynard

D-17   **THE GIRL WHO LOVED DEATH** by Paul W. Fairman
       SLAVE PLANET by Laurence M. Janifer

D-18   **SECOND CHANCE** by J. F. Bone
       MISSION TO A DISTANT STAR by Frank Belknap Long

D-19   **THE SYNDIC** by C. M. Kornbluth
       FLIGHT TO FOREVER by Poul Anderson

D-20   **SOMEWHERE I'LL FIND YOU** by Milton Lesser
       THE TIME ARMADA by Fox B. Holden

ARMCHAIR SCIENCE FICTION CLASSICS, $12.95 each

C-4   **CORPUS EARTHLING**
     by Louis Charbonneau

C-5   **THE TIME DISSOLVER**
     by Jerry Sohl

C-6   **WEST OF THE SUN**
     by Edgar Pangborn

ARMCHAIR SC-FI & HORROR GEMS SERIES, $12.95 each

G-1   **SCIENCE FICTION GEMS, Vol. One**
     Isaac Asimov and others

G-2   **HORROR GEMS, Vol. One**
     Carl Jacobi and others

If you've enjoyed this book, you will not want to miss these terrific titles…

ARMCHAIR SCI-FI & HORROR DOUBLE NOVELS, $12.95 each

D-31   **A HOAX IN TIME** by Keith Laumer
INSIDE EARTH by Poul Anderson

D-32   **TERROR STATION** by Dwight V. Swain
THE WEAPON FROM ETERNITY by Dwight V. Swain

D-33   **THE SHIP FROM INFINITY** by Edmond Hamilton
TAKEOFF by C. M. Kornbluth

D-34   **THE METAL DOOM** by David H. Keller
TWELVE TIMES ZERO by Howard Browne

D-35   **HUNTERS OUT OF SPACE** by Joseph Kelleam
INVASION FROM THE DEEP by Paul W. Fairman,

D-36   **THE BEES OF DEATH** by Robert Moore Williams
A PLAGUE OF PYTHONS by Frederick Pohl

D-37   **THE LORDS OF QUARMALL** by Fritz Leiber and Harry Fischer
BEACON TO ELSEWHERE by James H. Schmitz

D-38   **BEYOND PLUTO** by John S. Campbell
ARTERY OF FIRE by Thomas N. Scortia

D-39   **SPECIAL DELIVERY** by Kris Neville
NO TIME FOR TOFFEE by Charles F. Meyers

D-40   **JUNGLE IN THE SKY** by Milton Lesser
RECALLED TO LIFE by Robert Silverberg

ARMCHAIR SCIENCE FICTION CLASSICS, $12.95 each

C-10   **MARS IS MY DESTINATION**
by Frank Belknap Long

C-11   **SPACE PLAGUE**
by George O. Smith

C-12   **SO SHALL YE REAP**
by Rog Phillips

ARMCHAIR SCI-FI & HORROR GEMS SERIES, $12.95 each

G-3   **SCIENCE FICTION GEMS, Vol. Two**
James Blish and others

G-4   **HORROR GEMS, Vol. Two**
Joseph Payne Brennan and others